The Rose Weapon

F.C. Shultz

Front cover image by Timothy Rhyne on Unsplash
Front cover design by Logan Greer
Back cover image by Mark N Photography

This is a work of fiction. Names, characters, businesses, places, events and incidents are either the products of the author's imagination or used in a fictitious manner. Any resemblance to actual persons, living or dead, or actual events is purely coincidental.

for Sammi,
thank you for dreaming with me.

More stories available at
www.fcshultz.com

The
Rose
Weapon

1

The straw-filled beast used for target practice was nowhere near the size of the actual fire beast. The wingspan of the downed tree branches attached to the stuffed body made the imitation look frightening in the darkness of the early morning. Even still, Hosperan could manage a kill shot with his spear from anywhere on the training grounds.

The sun had just made its way over Mount Kondor, the tallest in the Northern range, by the time Hosperan had finished his morning endurance training. The beams hit the grassy field and gave him a second wind after the morning of training. The only shadow cast by a winged replica; straw and grass falling out of its puncture wounds.

Hosperan brought five spears, each varying in length, to the field. He enjoyed these days. When he arrived that morning, he had stabbed the silver spearheads in the tree stump about three hundred paces from the target. Holding the first one like an oversized dagger, he began to focus his aim. The smooth body of the spear touched the outside of his ear as a deep breath filled his lungs. "Hey Hasberoon," a voice screeched behind him. The spear flew past the target and stuck to a tree thirty yards its rear.

"What do you want, Agur. I'm training."

"Training for what? It's not like you're going to attack those weaklings in Ebeltoft. Ha! Can you see it guys, Hosperan using his toothpicks to actually do something good for our village." Agar's friends laughed. Hosperan's cousin was three years older than him, but his size didn't show it.

"Leave me alone," Hosperan said.

"You can't order me around. You aren't the chief. Anyway, my mother says I would make a far better chief than you. Most of the elders think that too. Even Svana."

"She does not," Hosperan protested. "And you know I didn't choose this. I don't even know what I'm doing."

"That's obvious," Agur replied.

"But I know I'm not going to be a chief who orders everyone to run and hide when the fire falls."

"You mean run around like a fool and die," Agur paused. "like your father did."

"My father was a hero!" Hosperan grabbed a spear from the stump and tackled Agur to the ground. Holding the spear in both hands he pressed it against Agur's neck. "My father's a hero," Hosperan repeated before Agur's friends pulled him off.

"He's a coward. And the prophecy isn't even about you. It could be about anyone. My father was the captain of the Kittla Seafarers. They raided more cities than anyone can count. And I'm just as skilled with the spear as you," Agur said as he lifted himself off the ground.

"Contest! Contest!" said one of Agur's friends.

"Yes! A competition," Agur said as he looked around. "Whoever can spear this apple off your stuffed target's head gets to be chief."

"And if I win, you leave me alone."

"Of course, cousin. Whatever you say."

One of the friends ran the apple out to the target. Agur picked up a few spears from the stump and tested their weight. After selecting one that met his standards, he took aim. A slight breeze swept the valley and Agur waited until it ceased. He took a deep breath. Seconds later the spear escaped his grasp toward the apple. The apple remained unmoved. No one said anything.

Agur picked up another spear, aimed, and released. This time pinning the spear to the tree behind with the apple pierced through. "Whatever. It's not like you can even hit the apple if you lived a thousand lives."

The friend raced out to replace the deceased apple. Hosperan already has his spear in his hand from when he pinned Agur moments before.

He took aim.

The friend's hand was still placing the apple when Hosperan's spear cut through the top of the fruit and pinned it against the tree behind. The spear also pierced the apple that had been pinned previously.

"You idiot! You could've killed me!" Agur's friend yelled across the field. Hosperan grabbed his remaining weaponry and walked back to the village.

He was late for the elders' meeting.

2

Hosperan dropped the weapons off at his house before making his way to The Great Hall.

The streets were awake by now. Parents were teaching children everything from sword fighting to the history of their people to the gods and their sacrifices. A bronze statue of the fire beast stood in the middle of town square. It's wings spread wide and it's head pointed toward the heavens. Hosperan overheard a father telling some children, "There is no reason to be afraid, my child. There is great honor in being taken by fire."

Hosperan shook his head slightly, but said nothing. It had never sat right with him. He never had peace with the beast like these children had been given. This was one of the reasons that led him to confront the elders so many times. And it is what led him to confront them today. He passed Svana's house, but decided not to stop. He needed to get to the meeting before it ended.

When he arrived, they had already begun, but they paused and welcomed him to his seat. Hosperan found his seat at the end of a battle-worn wood table. The table was reclaimed wood from a legendary ship Agur's father had captained.

"It is nice to see you, Hosperan." Ragnhild, an elder spokesman, said. "It has been awhile since you have joined us."

"I have something to bring to your attention, but I can wait until you have finished what was being discussed before I arrived."

"Nonsense, if the chief-to-be has a matter to discuss it must be of great importance. Unless it is the fire beast nonsense." The elders laughed. "All other matters must be postponed. Everyone in agreement?" The elders surrounding the tables shook their head in agreement accompanied by a booming "ja."

"That's the thing. You are being foolish. All of you." Hosperan said. "We need to prepare for the Night of Fire."

The faces surrounding him were jovial, and a few condescending laughs echoed off the walls, but no one said anything in response. Just as Hosperan was about to speak again, Ragnhild replied.

"Our apologies Hos, but what do you mean prepare? There is no preparing."

"I don't know. Figure it out. Let's reinforce our homes, hide our supplies, double our prayers," Hosperan took a deep breath before finishing. "Fight the beast."

"Don't be so stupid, child. We are mortal beings. There is no fighting the beast. That is like a bee taking on a whale," Ragnhild replied. Then an aged man from the end of the table spoke.

"Even if we could defeat the beast, why would we want to? It only claims the sacrifices the gods require. The gods do not ask much from us at all, yet they provide the harvest and the plunder."

"But it..."

"You haven't forgotten the divine order, have you? 'He who displays a malicious act toward the beast will be damned worse than an enemy.' I didn't make the rules Hos," Ragnhild replied.

"It cannot be right. My dreams. It is so...."

"Not with the dreams again," Ragnhild pleaded.

"It's suicide!" Hosperan stood out of his seat. "If we knew the Ebeltoftons were planning an attack we would not retreat to our homes and wait for our destruction."

"When your father was chief we would have," murmured someone from around the table.

"Who said that? As chief I demand you identify yourself," Hosperan declared.

"You are not chief yet Hosperan. Not until your birthday. Then your father's shield will be yours." Ragnhild pointed to a shield that hung on the wall. "Ten more days, is it?"

"Very well. I'll make sure to have you all replaced when I become chief." Hosperan stormed out of the meeting place without looking back. He heard whispering as he left, but paid them no attention. He needed to find someone he could talk to; someone who would listen to him and care about what he had to say. He needed to find his best friend Gildor.

3

Hosperan left the meeting place and headed south toward the fields. He knew he would find his friend there. Gildor was a farmer by trade and an orphan by fate. Both of his parents died ten years ago during the last Night of Fire; same as Hosperan's father. The road leading out of town had transitioned from dirt to weeds to a grassy path. Hosperan saw his friend sitting under a tree.

"What is this? Sleeping on the job? I won't have it! The chief needs his ale immediately," Hosperan said.

"Well when the chief gets here I'll make sure to get it for him," Gildor smiled and replied.

"Ha, you little," at this Hosperan tackled his friend and they wrestled under the tree, laughing as they jockeyed for dominance. Gildor was easy to pin down and defeat, but Hosperan let the wrestling match go on for the sport of it and to let his friend feel like he won. When he decided to pin Gildor it was over in a matter of seconds.

"I almost had you that time, Hosperan."

"I'm a little stronger than those pigs you've been wrestling," replied the victor. "I've seen you practicing out here."

"It's the closest thing I've got that resembles you."

F.C. SHULTZ

Gildor was never short on jokes. He had loved teasing Hosperan since they were children. But there was a certain maturity he could display at a moment's notice.

"What brings you to the fields this early? You're usually at the training ground all morning," Gildor asked.

"Agur and his insects showed up and started trouble. But I wish you could've seen it. He challenged me to a spear throwing contest."

"What an idiot," Gildor said.

"Right? He set up an apple about forty yards out and he took his time, set his aim, and then missed."

"Ha, serves him right."

"And he told me 'Whoever wins gets to be chief,' which means absolutely nothing. It's not like I'm choosing this."

"So, did you win?"

"Oh yeah. He missed his first throw and then picked up another spear and hit the target the second time. Then as one of his friends was setting up the next apple for me I threw my spear and pinned it while it was still in his hand."

"What! You filthy fox!"

"Honestly, I was a little surprised I actually did it. I didn't show my surprise of course.

"I bet the fifl placing the apple was pissed."

"Oh yeah, he was yelling and cursing me. That's not even the best part though."

"Well, go on."

"Agur's second spear had pinned the apple to the tree behind the target. When I threw my spear it not only pinned my apple to the tree but it also went through his apple as well. Two for one!"

"No way, man. You're full of fish food."

"I swear, it's probably still there."

"I've got to see this for myself."

With this, Gildor leapt to his feet and started making his way back through town toward the training ground. Hosperan followed.

"So, you came out here after your spear theatrics?" Gildor asked. They reached the dirt road on the edge of town. The trees overhead shook with the wind. The sunlight danced on the path before them as the breeze made its way through the leaves.

"Well, I stopped by the elders' meeting on my way to see you."

"Why?"

"The dreams. I'm having the dreams again. My father is there, burning, holding me, pleading with me to honor him. I don't know what that means. I wanted the elders to help me. To help me do something," Hosperan said.

"Like what?" Gildor asked.

"Like help me fight the beast."

"That's not allowed," Gildor took a breath. "Do you think that would help? With the honoring?"

"I don't know. I don't know how to honor him."

"Can I tell you something, Hos."

"Of course."

"Whenever I don't know what to do, I try and figure out what my parents would do in the situation. My father always knew what to do. He was a farmer and he was planning on applying for the eldership. And if he didn't know what to do, my mother definitely did."

"How does that," Hosperan held his tongue. He looked at his friend and continued as gentle as he could. "So, you're saying I should try and figure out what my father would do if he was having dreams that his father was asking for honor?"

"Well, uh." Gildor dropped his head. "I'm just trying to help, Hos."

"I know, I know. I'm sorry. I didn't mean it like that. I think it's great advice." Hosperan didn't say anything for a short while. They both walked in silence through town. People waved and they waved back. Then Hosperan spoke up.

"Okay, you're right. I need to figure out what my father would do to honor someone who died saving him. He is reaching out to me through my dreams. I can't let his death be just another sacrifice. It isn't right. But there's a problem."

"What's that?"

"I don't know much about my father. Most of the legends seem too fantastic to be true."

"You need to talk to people who knew him."

"The storyteller," Hosperan lifted his head. "He knew my father well."

"Well you can't go just yet, I need to see this double apple evidence for myself."

They reached the training ground and crossed the field. When they came to the forest's edge, Gildor spoke up.

"Where are these spears and apples?"

"Agur must have taken them with him. You can see the two holes here though," Hosperan said as he pointed at the two piercings in the tree.

"Ahh, I don't believe it. I'm going to go ask Agur," Gildor said with a laugh.

"Oh yeah, I'm sure he'll tell you exactly what happened," Hosperan replied.

"Well, I better head back to my field and finish the day's harvest. I have to make sure I have everything ready for tonight."

"Sounds good. Thank you for your help, friend."

"Of course, friend." They grabbed hands like a standing arm wrestle was about to take place. Then they bowed their heads for a second. Afterwards, Gildor punched Hosperan in the arm and said, "Got you last," and then ran off in the direction of his field, laughing all the way. Hosperan returned home for a moment to get some lunch before heading to talk to the storyteller. His mother was sitting outside waiting for him to return.

4

"Where have you been?"

"Mother, you know I go to the training ground in the morning."

"Yes, but the elders' council got out of session an hour ago and I heard you caused quite a problem in there."

"Can we go inside to talk. I need some food." His mother did not consent verbally, but she picked herself up and went inside while he held the door open. Inside, Hosperan began to cook over the fire.

"Why are you causing problems, Hosperan?"

"I'm not causing problems, Mother. I'm pointing out the problems that already exist. It's not right. Why would the gods want the greatest chief that ever lived to be sacrificed? It doesn't make sense."

"Hosperan, please. We don't question these things. You need to stop with this madness. The elders are not happy with you. They are talking about calling for an election. Do you really want your cousin, Agur, to be chief? We need this."

"We? This is about you and your power. Have you even thought about me? I can't lead these people. What would Father do? I need to be more like him. I need to learn more about him."

"You want to know what he was like? He was soft. He refused to attack surrounding villages, which left us vulnerable. He didn't establish us as a threat. We were seen as weak. He spent time building new homes, all while neglecting this one. He was a selfish man. That is why the beast chose him as a sacrifice; to cleanse us of his filth."

"How dare you speak of him like that. He did many great things. Everyone loved him."

"Don't be naive, child. He was no leader. He was born a farmer. You're the one who will fulfill the prophecy."

"Enough with the prophecy," Hosperan said as he threw his plate on the ground. He knew he had gone too far. "I'm sorry, Mother." His mother didn't respond. "It's just too much. What if I can't live up to the prophecy? What if I can't live up to Father's legacy? I don't know how to be a chief. I don't know how to lead these people. I don't know how to honor the dead who were sacrificed before me. I need to find out what Father would do. I need guidance. I want to lead these people, but no one has shown me how," Hosperan stood and walked toward the door. "I am going to talk to the storyteller. I will be back later. I love you, Mother."

His mother stood and wrapped her hand around the back of his head, like she was holding a newborn. She looked at him, but no words came out. He left the house and made his way to the storyteller's dwelling.

The storyteller would be able to tell Hosperan all about his father. He was the record keeper. And he had recalled stories about Hosperan's father at various times in the past. That is what Hosperan needed now; a reminder of who his father was and how he acted. But he wouldn't get that just yet.

When Hosperan arrived at the small home in the middle of town, no one was home. The house was empty. The dwelling looked older than the storyteller himself and somehow had never been destroyed by the fire beast in nights past. But Hosperan didn't care much for architecture. He was on a mission.

The streets were still as lively as earlier that morning. A group of young boys were carrying logs from the edge of the forest to the town square. Others were setting up stumps and chairs around the stacked wood, while some began to work on igniting the fire. A small group of people were sitting in the shade of the fire beast's bronze wings, fiddling with something in their hands. He walked over to see what they were doing.

Once he got closer it dawned on him; they were carving small figures representing the loved ones who had been sacrificed by the beast. They would need these later. Hosperan decided to sit down and join them. No words were spoken. Someone handed him a piece of wood slightly larger than his hand and a small knife the size of his finger. He spent the rest of the afternoon carving the man he had seen in his dreams.

He finished just as the Festival of Fire began.

5

The fire circled the bronze fire beast and raged above the housetops. Every member of the village had found their place around the flames. People were three or four deep in most places. From where Hosperan was sitting, he could not see the people directly across from him because the fire had grown so large. He could see Svana about a quarter way around the circle. She waved at him and he waved back. Gildor was in the same area. He made a fist at Hosperan and laughed.

The people were talking amongst themselves. The voices were a low murmur above the crackling of the fire. Hosperan's seat was reserved for the chief, but the elders insisted that he sit there tonight with his mother beside him while they surrounded on either side.

A man with burned clothes made his way to the fire. A hood combined with the shadows cast from the shifting fire made it impossible to make out any facial features. By the pace at which he walked, it appeared that his leg was wounded. As he approached the fire, the murmurs stopped. The only sound came from the lighted heat, which they all surrounded and feared. Then he began.

"When man was first brought forth into the world, it was not without great cost. The gods took a piece of themselves and used that as a seed for man. That is why we are called 'Hankar' or 'of the gods.' But this was not without great price.

What price can be paid to satisfy the ones who created you? Oh, what great debt. No gift of man can satisfy except for man himself. And, still, a small price to pay. For once every ten years the fire beast is sent to collect what is due. To select sacrifices from among their creation. And even so doing are sacrificing themselves over and over again.

So tonight, we honor those who have paid the price to satisfy our gods and we prepare ourselves for our own possible sacrifice. May the fire beast breathe his cleansing flames and may our souls satisfy the gods demands."

The sound of drums and singing began as the man finished his last word. All people began to celebrate. Women and men danced with their children and neighbors around the fire. The meal consisted of a thousand flundra; which appeared to be about half of that amount by now. All the while, the flames reached toward the heavens and Hosperan sat in his chair holding his carved image.

He was shaken back to reality when the elders quieted the crowds and signaled that they had an announcement to make. They were surrounding Hosperan. Sitting up straight, he counted the elders around him.

Seven.

They were all there. It did not appear that there was danger present. They definitely would not try anything stupid at the Feast of Fire; not with the entire village around. Hosperan eased back in his chair slightly and exhaled a half-breath. Ragnhild began to speak.

"As you know, we have been without a true chief since the last Night of Fire nearly ten years ago. The eldership and I have satisfied the requirements and responsibilities of a chief with glad hearts. We want you all to survive and thrive in this land."

The village cheered.

"But this is not how our villages have been designed to operate. And we, the people of Kilbo, are in the midst of trying times. Our crops are drying up and our livestock are thin. We need a leader. A chief must reign supreme. A chief must guide. A chief must be wholly focused on the well-being of the people and must confess and share the beliefs that have been passed down from our fathers and our fathers' fathers before them.

There is a boy who is next in line to fulfill these duties. As you all know, Hosperan will reach manhood on his sixteenth birthday in just ten days' time. On that day, the chiefdom and all of its' responsibilities will be bestowed upon his shoulders."

Hosperan couldn't believe what he was hearing. Could these be the same men he debated with earlier in the day. What had changed since this morning? He sat still in his chair as Ragnhild finished.

"So please, show your gratitude and appreciation for your new chief, Hosperan the Geirdle." The entire village roared with applause and cheering. Ragnhild motioned for Hosperan to stand and acknowledge the crowd.

"Thank you," Hosperan said in a voice inaudible to anyone farther than an arm's reach. Ragnhild came over and hugged Hosperan. But when Hosperan tried to release, Ragnhild was still holding tight. With their heads side-by-side Ragnhild whispered into Hosperan's ear and said, "Don't get comfortable."

6

Hosperan stared at Ragnhild as the elders made their way back to their seats. He was the only one still standing as the storyteller walked toward the fire. All eyes were on the soon to be chief. When his mother noticed that Hosperan was still standing, she tugged on his arm and motioned to sit down. Hosperan sat forward in his chair without taking his eyes off Ragnhild. The storyteller began to speak.

"The reason for this festival is to remember those who have been sacrificed so that we may keep on living. It is an act that cannot be repaid, and never forgotten. I am here to recall the stories from the lives of the sacrificed. And what better way to start than by remembering our great chief, Hosperan's father, Raknar the Valiant."

Hosperan's focus shifted instantly at the mention of his father's name. The words of Ragnhild seemed a wisp compared to the storyteller's speech.

"This man befriended our enemies nearby, and, thus opened new trade-routes. We were attacked little and we attacked little. All had plenty and none without. The time of plenty, the thirty-three years of his reign, were the greatest that these people have ever enjoyed. We show our appreciation by remembering him today." The storyteller bowed his head and the surrounding crowd followed. The fire crackled as the village fell silent for a moment.

"As the keeper of the stories for the sacrificed, there are none that rival this man. But perhaps he is most known for his architectural superiority." Hosperan had taken the carved statue out of his bag and was holding it in his hand as the storyteller spoke.

"All who are here have benefitted from the homes he helped construct. In his short lifetime, he took us from wood to stone. From darkness to light. His fingerprint is evident all over the village. But his renown does not stop there.

He was known to be the last to enter his home after the fire beast arrived. He was deeply religious and believed that the mind and soul should be prepared if the beast decides to take your body for sacrifice. In his first Night of Fire, as a nine year old, before he was the chief of course, he was running home after the beast had attacked, when he heard a scream.

A toddler was trapped under a flaming tree branch that had fallen. The flaming cage trapped the child inside. Raknar reached into the flames and pulled the child out. The child ran home unscathed, save singed hair. But Raknar was not as fortunate.

His entire arm had caught fire.

The flesh melted off of the muscle and the blood beneath boiled. He ran to the stream in the forest and submerged the mutilated arm. His arm became scarred like the skin of the fire beast. He would never forget that night. I believe that is what drove him to greatness all the way until his last night in this world.

On the last Night of Fire, nearly ten years ago, the fire beast came early. It came unexpected. No one was ready. Raknar went above and beyond to make sure everyone was able to get to their homes. He grabbed an empty barrel and began to bang his sword against the side. The sound of metal on wood rose louder than the sound of flames licking branches off trees. He ran through the forest and up the riverbank. The beast followed close behind.

Raknar's body was never found. A short time later this barrel was found lodged against the bank of the river, just outside of the village. The top half completely charred and the other broken from being slapped against rocks whilst riding the rapids home."

As the storyteller was saying this, he held up a small piece of wood. It would have been unrecognizable as being a barrel had the storyteller not shared its origin.

"Your father was a great man. And there are few others who have had as great an influence on this village. Our sixth chief, Torun No-Jafn, moved us from the inland and founded our beloved village Kilbo."

The storyteller went on, but Hosperan could not focus on anything except the carved image in his hand. He imagined it leading the beast away. He imagined the bravery required to do something like that; the quick-thinking, the strength.

The storyteller concluded his tales of those who had been sacrificed.

"It is now time to honor those who have gone before. Those who have paid the price so that we may continue to live. Those who have been cleansed by the flame. May we never forget."

As he concluded, each member of the village who had lost someone to the fire beast stood and approached the fire. Each person had their own carved image of the ones they had lost. And each took their carved image and tossed it into the fire to be consumed again as a symbol of their sacrifice. Hosperan saw Svana and Gildor approach the flames.

As Hosperan approached the fire, he could not do it. The connection was too strong. It did not feel right to him. It did not feel okay. The wooden figure would not let go of him. So, he stood next to the fire and took his dagger from his waist and tossed it to the flames. He filled the void in his sheath with the wooden memory of his father.

The Feast of Fire continued until deep into the night. Hosperan retired early to his bed; where the dreams intensified. The storyteller's tales manifested in his subconscious that night.

7

A cage of fire surrounded him on all sides. There was nowhere to go; and even less space to move. The branches of a flaming tree had fallen and knocked him to the ground. The fire beast flew overhead and the moon disappeared for a moment. A cry echoed off the mountains. Hosperan knew he would die here.

Then the sound of feet treading through leaves grew louder and louder. Someone was running toward him. Although the fire was burning an intense heat, the glow was absent. There was just darkness surrounding.

"Help me! Sir! Please, I'm stuck," Hosperan said in a voice he hadn't heard for nearly ten years. "I can't die here. I'm too young."

The sound of stomping feet was the loudest it had yet been. The being had to be near.

A figure emerged from the forest, but it was no man. No person of any kind. It was the wooden statue that Hosperan had carved earlier that day. It did not say a word. It seemed to have its own source of light coming from within. The figure reached its arm into the fiery entrapment and pulled Hosperan out. The wooden arm caught fire and was nearly incinerated by the time it spread to his wooden body.

The flames overtook the carved image.

The wooden man reached down and picked Hosperan up and cried, "Honor me, honor me."

After a moment, the man threw Hosperan to the ground. The sensation of falling backwards jolted him awake.

Hosperan was in his bed.

The small statue sitting next to his bed with it's gaze fixed directly on him. Hosperan tried to go back to sleep, but "Honor me" echoed in his mind the rest of the night. He had to visit the storyteller in the morning.

8

Hosperan skipped breakfast and his morning training in order to arrive at the storyteller's dwelling as soon as possible. The storyteller was not awake when Hosperan arrived, so he waited outside for a short time before trying again. He considered going to check on Svana while he was waiting. It had been a few days since they last spoke. While he was considering this, the door to the storyteller's house cracked open.

"Hosperan, you are here early," the storyteller said as he opened the door wider. He motioned for his guest to come inside. The storyteller sat in his seat next to an ember fire.

"I know. I'm sorry. It's about my father. I need to know more," Hosperan said as he found a wooden stool and moved it in front of the storyteller with only a small gap between.

"What do you want to know? I don't know all, of course. But I know some. Mostly good. I don't remember the bad things as well. But I did know Raknar his entire life."

"There are so many things. I don't know where to start. I barely remember him. And I'm sure my memories are not memories at all, but the combination of the stories I've heard from others."

"Are those things separate? Memories and stories from others," the storyteller questioned.

"Well, they aren't my memories. How can I trust them? How can I believe them?" Hosperan said.

"If you trust the people telling you the stories, then you can believe them, right? You believed the stories I told of your father last night, correct? I suppose you wouldn't be here otherwise."

"Well, yes."

"And I shared a memory with you. And now you have it as your own. You didn't experience it as it happened, but now you can share it with others."

"It feels strange to combine my experiences with the experiences of others and call them the same. I wouldn't make a spear and then take a sword from you and call the sword a spear. Those are different."

"Ah, you are thinking too small. You would not call them both spears, that would be foolish. But you would call them both weapons," the storyteller said as he leaned forward in his chair. "If we were to go to battle you would not care much if you had the spear you made or the sword I forged and gifted to you. Both would be useful in the time of need."

"Yes of course. Anything can become a weapon, can become useful if necessary."

"Exactly," the storyteller said as he sat back in his chair and relaxed.

"What does this have to do with my father?"

"Exactly," the storyteller repeated.

Hosperan was not amused with the storyteller's ambiguity, but he chose to suppress the frustration. Hosperan wanted answers. He wanted guidance. He wanted direction. After a few moments of silence, he spoke again.

"I've been having dreams of my father."

"That's interesting. Go on," the storyteller insisted.

"It's always the Night of Fire. The trees are burning, the houses are burning, everything is burning. And right when I'm in trouble, right when the beast is going to make me a sacrifice, my father shows up and takes the heat. He bears the fire. His flaming self is always before me, clutching my shoulders, repeating the same words, 'Honor me, honor me.'"

"Hmmph," was the storyteller's only response.

"I guess that's why I'm here. I don't know how to honor him. I don't know how to respect the deceased. What does that even mean?"

"That's a great question," the storyteller said.

"I came to you because I thought you could help me. Because you knew him better than I ever will."

"Ah, but he is no longer living. It seems you know him much better now. And he is calling out to you. I am a storyteller, not a mystic."

"Please, help me. The dreams. The pain every night," Hosperan said as he wiped his eyes.

"I do have one suggestion."

"Please, anything."

"Have you visited the memorial grounds of the sacrificed recently? Up past Mount Kondor."

"No, I haven't," Hosperan paused. "Not since the memorial service after his death."

"Go. Travel to the mountains and visit his memorial. Spend some time there and see what he says."

Hosperan thought this a brilliant idea. Not only did he feel this a great way to honor his father, but he could use an escape from the village for a short time. He would ask Gildor to accompany him. They always had great adventures when they were boys. This would be an excellent last adventure before Hosperan was thrust into the responsibility that chiefdom brings.

"Thank you. This is excellent. I have great peace about this. I'll leave at once," Hosperan said as he began to get to his feet.

"Of course, Hosperan. Anything for the chief-to-be. I hope you find what you are searching for," the storyteller said as Hosperan made his way to the door.

"Thank you again," Hosperan said as he closed the door behind him and made his way home to prepare for the journey. His mother would not think this a very good plan. Hosperan hoped she was not home when he arrived.

His hope did not come true.

"I'm going to the memorial grounds of the sacrificed. I'm leaving right now." Hosperan decided there was no reason to try and avoid the inevitable. He had just walked in the door of his house when he announced his plans.

"You're what? I don't think so. People will think that you have abandoned the village. If the fire beast shows up, you will be considered a shameful svikr. You won't be allowed back," his mother said. She paused, and then said, "You won't be chief."

"You mean we won't be chief," Hosperan replied. "This whole thing is about you. It is about you staying in power. Do you even care about me? About my well-being?"

"Of course, I do, Son. But the prophecy is clear that..."

"I don't care about the stupid prophecy," Hosperan interrupted. "And if you really did care about me, you would let me do this." Hosperan began to put a few items into a small sack. "It's only a day's journey. If the people ask, tell them I am making a sacrifice to the gods. They won't question you."

"Why do you need to go? What is the point? I don't understand."

"I don't expect you to understand. And I don't need you to understand. I will be back the day after tomorrow." He finished packing a few small rations; his sword, spear, cask, and his pelt outer layer.

His mother grabbed his arm in an attempt to make him stay. "Please stay with me," his mother begged.

"There's no reason to stay," Hosperan replied. He ripped his arm out of her grasp and left the house. He just needed to find Gildor and then he would be ready to go.

9

"What's gnawing your ankles?" Gildor asked.

"Nothing really," Hosperan replied. "My mother. She's mad."

"She doesn't want you to go to the memorial grounds?"

"She doesn't think it's necessary."

"Hmm."

"Don't tell me you're on her side too."

"I'm not on anyone's side, I'm just trying to think like her."

"Don't waste your time. It'll make you crazy," Hosperan replied. "Are we ready to go?"

"I think so," Gildor said. "You don't want to say bye to Svana?"

"It's only a day's journey, man."

"And?"

"It doesn't matter." Hosperan paused. "Let's go."

They made their way toward the forest north of the village. People were cleaning up the dead embers from the night before. Others were bringing in crops from the fields. School lessons were in session. A group of young ones were walking toward Hosperan and Gildor. They were being led by their teacher.

Svana.

"Hi Hosperan. You boys going somewhere?"

"We're going to the memorial grounds," Gildor answered. Hosperan tightened his eyes and looked at his friend.

"Oh," Svana said as her head dropped.

"Do you mind if I do some show and tell with your class? I've got a necklace that I think they will like." Gildor stepped aside and addressed the class. "What do you all think? Can I show you something cool?"

All the children cheered.

"All right. But only for a moment," Svana responded. Gildor led the class out of earshot and then sat down with them in a circle.

"You didn't tell me you were leaving the village," Svana said without skipping a beat.

"Do I have to tell you every time I make a decision?"

"Hosperan."

"What? It's only a day's journey."

"It's not about that. You're just unbelievable sometimes. You know that?" Hosperan didn't respond right away. Svana turned away from him and faced Mount Kondor.

"I need to go or we won't make it in time," he said to break the silence.

"Okay, do what you need to do." She wiped her face. "I'll be here, waiting. Like always."

Hosperan made a hand motion to Gildor and he finished up his story and led the class back to their teacher. The two groups went their separate ways.

It wasn't long before they were on the edge of the village. Hosperan took one last look before they traveled on the east road through the forest. Then he faced forward and looked up to the cloud-piercing mountain to the left of him.

"The memorial is just on the other side of Mount Kondor. Should we circle around the flatlands or take the mountain pass?" Hosperan asked.

"You don't want to talk about what just happened?" Gildor replied.

"No. No I don't."

"Okay then." Gildor gathered his thoughts before continuing. "Well, the flatlands take longer, right? I'm not trying to be gone all week."

"It's longer, but it's easier. Because it's flat. The land is flat."

"I know what flat means," Gildor said. "But isn't it close to a lynx hunting ground?"

"I don't know. But the mountain pass is cold. Like, snow cold."

"But there's a fjord just off the mountain pass. I wouldn't mind going for a swim."

"Then it's settled. The mountain pass it is. The water is going to be freezing though."

"Hopefully you remember how to make a fire then."

"You're insane," Hosperan laughed.

The road they traveled was just wide enough for two people. It wound through the forest to avoid the larger trees, but the path was littered with small stump remains that could not compete with the axes of men. After traveling for a short time, they turned north and abandoned the flatlands.

"What gave you the idea to visit the memorial grounds? Especially during fire season," Gildor asked.

"Well, you know the dreams I've been telling you about?"

"With your dad asking you to respect him or something?"

"Yeah. Well, he says 'Honor me,'" Hosperan said.

"Is there a difference?" Gildor asked.

"I don't know," Hosperan said and then paused for a moment before going on. "He shakes me and says 'Honor me. Honor me.' and I have no idea how."

"So, we're going to pay our respects...err honors."

"Well yesterday you said when you don't know what to do, you try and figure out what your parents would do in the same situation. I thought that was brilliant."

"Thank you, thank you. You can pay me later."

"Ha, I'm serious. So, I went to talk to the storyteller. He knew my father well."

"And?" Gildor asked.

"He gave me the idea to visit the memorial grounds."

"And you waited all of two hours before leaving?" Gildor said with a grin.

"Oh, axe off. What else was I going to do? Why wait?" Hosperan replied.

"I'm just giving you a hard time. I wouldn't have waited either. Well I didn't, because you asked me an hour ago. And here we are."

"Here we are."

They had begun the slow climb up the south side of Mount Kondor. The path was made from the dirt under less committed rocks that had been moved aside. There was no snow yet, but they could see the white powder ahead. They came to a small overlook and decided to take a break. The treetops were visible from the rock where they rested.

"I really thought we'd be higher than this by now," Hosperan said, looking at the sun approaching the ocean.

"Worried about the fire beast coming while we're gone?" Gildor asked.

"Well, yeah."

"We'd be shameful svikrs. Weird."

"You seem oddly at peace with that idea," Hosperan said.

"Well, I would just go somewhere else. Kilbo is not much of a home. No family. Only a few friends. Mostly just acquaintances though. And I can farm anywhere. You're really the only thing that keeps me there. And if I get shamefully svikred then you do too," Gildor said with a laugh.

"Thank you, I think," Hosperan shared in the laughter. "I'm mostly concerned about my mother. If the fire beast does come, she would be alone."

"I thought you said she let the 'you being chief' thing go to her head."

"She has. I think. It seems like it's all she talks about. She wants the power. But she's still my mother. That has to mean something, right?"

"I think so," Gildor said.

"Me too," Hosperan replied. He was getting ready to grab his sack and start moving again when Gildor spoke.

"You want to know something?"

"Of course."

"I travel to the memorial grounds every year. I spend a few days at the memorial site, talking to stones with my parents' names on them. I give them updates on my life and what is going on around the village," Gildor paused. "But this year I didn't. I decided I wasn't going to go; that it was a child's errand. I thought it foolish to talk to stones."

"That's not foolish, Gildor. That is incredible."

"How so?"

"It shows how much they mean to you. To care enough to make the trip and spend time there."

"You don't think it is a bit pathetic? Sometimes I question if I have ever accepted the fact that they are gone. I've never let them go."

"Who says you have to let them go? Not completely anyway. I think it's a great tribute to them. And that they would be proud. That they are proud."

"Thanks, Hos. For inviting me to join you."

"I really just wanted someone to talk to on the trip, but you're welcome." After Hosperan said this, Gildor shoved him off of the rock where they were sitting. They both started laughing. They gathered themselves, picked up their sacks, and made their way back to the path.

Hosperan thought about how his friend had honored his parents and wondered if he could do the same. Questions echoed in his mind as they traveled. It was not long until the dirt rock path turned snow covered and revealed another set of footprints traveling the same direction as them.

10

"It's just a fox," Hosperan said.

"Well, it's definitely not human. But I don't think it's a fox," Gildor replied.

"Why not?"

"They're too big. But it is definitely four legged."

"Obviously," Hosperan said.

"It could be a lynx," Gildor whispered.

The snow fell in small flakes like dust settling after a breeze. Hosperan and Gildor followed the tracks up until they deviated from the mountain pass.

"Lynx don't come this high up the mountain. There's nothing to hunt," Hosperan said.

"I don't know," Gildor hesitated.

"Well, what do you say we do? We can't go back the flat lands route. Let's just make sure to keep a closer watch. It will be fine. And they aren't even the same direction as us. See, there's no more on the path."

Gildor hesitated. It looked as though he was in deep thought, weighing his options.

"Isn't the fjord just ahead? I'll race you to it. Last one in the water has to carry both our sacks the rest of the way," Hosperan said as he took off in a sprint up the mountain. He intentionally kicked snow up at Gildor to try and distract him.

They came to the mouth of the path and found a large body of water, clear as spring air, waiting for them. Hosperan shed his clothes and jumped into the fjord just ahead of Gildor. For that moment, Hosperan forgot all about mothers and fathers and chiefdoms and elders and fire beasts. He was lost in the nostalgia of the carefree days of his childhood. He shed his worry with his clothes and that lack of responsibility kept him afloat in the ice water all afternoon.

The sun was no longer visible through the trees when they stepped out of the fjord. They put their clothes back on by moonlight.

"We should make camp for the night," Gildor suggested.

"And, get a fire going to warm up. How much farther do you think we have?"

"Well, the fjord is a little over halfway. So, we're getting there."

"Whatever you say, Master of The Mountain."

"Thank you, thank you. Now, there is a small cleft in the mountain on the bank of this fjord. We can camp there."

"All hail Gildor, the magnificent travel guide," Hosperan said, as he bowed to one knee.

"Oh, get up. Let's find it quick. I'm hungry."

They grabbed their sacks and began to circle the water. The moon provided enough light that Hosperan considered traveling through the night. But he knew his friend was tired from the day's journey.

It did not take long to find Gildor's cleft and get a fire going. Hosperan was able to catch a few fish in the moonlight. They had settled in and began to eat their meal.

"Your fish is bigger than mine," Gildor said.

"Well, I'm bigger than you," Hosperan replied.

"Yeah, but. Well…" Gildor didn't respond.

"Ha, no comeback to that one huh?"

"Give me a minute, I'll think of something. At least give me some more loaf to make up for the difference."

Hosperan reached into his bag to grab some loaf for Gildor. The carved image of his father fell near the fire before them. They looked up at each other in an instant.

"Is that…" Gildor asked.

"Yes," Hosperan said with his head lowered. "I couldn't do it. I couldn't throw it in the fire."

"Hos, it's ritual. It's required."

"I know, I know. It just didn't feel right. Like he wouldn't let go of me."

"You mean, you wouldn't let go of him."

"Yeah. That's what I said." Hosperan picked up the statue and held it in his hands. "Can I tell you something?"

"Of course," Gildor replied.

"I think something has to be done about the fire beast." No one spoke. Gildor looked confused. The top log burned through and rolled to the side before Gildor's voice broke the silence.

"What do you mean?"

"I don't know. I think it's the only way to honor my father."

"But the ban. You'll be banned. It's not allowed. What about being chief? We need a good chief."

"I want to be a good chief. But I don't know if it's enough."

"But, the gods, they…"

"It doesn't make sense, though. The gods created us, right? They made us from a piece of themselves."

"Yeah."

"Then why would they want us to die? Why do they need us to die? It doesn't make sense."

"It just is. That's history. The storytellers have been passing down that history since the beginning. It's just the way it is."

"It can't be," Hosperan stood up. "It can't be right."

"So, you want to kill the beast. To kill tradition. How?"

"I don't know. I have no idea," Hosperan began to pace. "I need to plan. I need to study the beast. I need to find it's weakness."

"But it could come tomorrow."

"There's not enough time before this Night of Fire. But, if I make it through the cleansing, I'll have ten years to prepare. To study. To recruit." Hosperan sat back down next to the fire and looked at his friend.

"I don't expect you to join me. It's insanity, I know. Denying the gods. All I ask is that you keep my secret."

"Of course," Gildor said as he looked at his friend. "I won't fight with you, but we can always share a meal."

"Thank you," Hosperan said. He turned his gaze back to the figure in his hand, and then back to the fire. No one spoke the rest of the evening. Hosperan was deep in thought with the weight of denying history laying heavy on his clarity. The fire had turned to ember and both friends were on the cusp of sleep when they were startled awake by an unwelcoming sound.

A series of low growls rolled across the water.

11

The growls grew in intensity. Hosperan and Gildor were both on their feet. Gildor snatched up his dagger and Hosperan gripped his spear. The embers provided little light and the moon was now covered by clouds. Hosperan could not see more than a spear's length in front of him. The growls echoed louder and louder.

"Gildor," Hosperan whispered, "come over here by me. We need to get our backs to the wall of the cleft. You're too exposed."

"I can barely see. Where are you?"

"To your left, just a couple…" Hosperan was interrupted by the sound of his friend crying for help.

"Hos!" The cry was mixed with the sound of growls and hisses coming from all around them. Hosperan could feel the ground shaking. Animals on all fours where smothering his friend.

"Gildor!" Hosperan cried as he drove the end of his spear into one of the animals clawing his friend. He lifted the animal off the ground and tossed it next to the fire.

It was a lynx.

As he prepared for his next attack, the front paws of an animal met his face and knocked him to the ground. Blood escaped off the tip of his nose and the brute mounted him with fatal intentions. Hosperan held his spear in front of his body to provide a moment of protection. Then he extended his elbows to maneuver the animal on the ground beside him. All of this was done without opening his eyes.

Because he could not open his eyes.

He tried to stand, but failed. He felt light headed and weak. He was not sure how long he had been lying on the ground when his left eye opened for a moment. All he could see were blurry shadows before him.

A tall figure used a small blade to pierce the side of a lynx and then it grabbed the carcass of the deceased animal with both hands and threw it into two lynxes feeding a few feet away. Hosperan couldn't keep his eye open any longer.

When he woke in the morning, he had a patch over his right eye.

12

Only his left eye would open.

His heart was beating under the patch. The pain shot through the eye cavity directly into the brain. It took him a few moments to remember where he was, and who he was.

The fire from the night before had been stoked into flame with some kind of meat cooking above it.

Gildor was not in sight.

Hosperan lifted the patch to look out of both eyes and a strange voice called out and said, "I wouldn't do that."

"What," Hosperan said as he replaced the patch and turned behind him. There was a man standing on the edge of the fjord. A small raft floated beside him with what looked like weapons and supplies. "Where is my friend? Where is Gildor?"

"You are not the least bit concerned with who I am?" said the man.

"Why would I be? It's obvious you mean me no harm. You could have killed me as I slept," Hosperan said as he stood.

"Smart boy," the man replied.

"I need to find my friend. We were attacked by a pack of lynx last night," Hosperan said.

"I know. Filthy kottrs."

"That was, that was you fighting them."

"Yes."

"I thought it to be Gildor." Hosperan began to look around. "Gildor!" He shouted. "Gildor!"

"He can't hear you, child."

"Has he gone back to the village? To get help?"

"I'm afraid not."

"Where is my friend?"

The stranger pointed to the makeshift raft. Now that Hosperan was standing, he could see there was something else on the raft other than weapons and supplies.

A body wrapped in cloths and placed on the raft.

Hosperan immediately ran into the water. The decline of the fjord floor was so steep that when Hosperan stood next to the raft only his shoulders were out of the water.

He folded back the cloth covering the head of the body.

Gildor.

Hosperan could barely recognize his friend. The claws of the lynx had torn through his cheek and into his gums, revealing the roots of his upper teeth. His eye cavity was vacant and his nose was now under this left eye.

Hosperan vomited in the water.

He covered his friend's face and then placed his own head on the chest of the deceased.

Then he wept.

"I should not have brought you. I know you are not a warrior. You are a farmer. This was a dangerous journey. A selfish quest. And now look what has happened."

The entire day passed with Hosperan standing in the water holding the shell of his friend. Hosperan could no longer feel his legs. He struggled to speak. The stranger stood on the shoreline in reverence.

"I'm ssssorry Gildorrrr," Hosperan said, shivering as the sun descended behind the edge of the mountain. "I am sssssooo ssssssorry." The raft trembled from its contact with Hosperan's body.

"Is it time?" asked the stranger.

"I guess so," Hosperan responded.

The stranger walked back toward the fire as Hosperan walked the raft to the edge of the shore. The man returned and handed Hosperan a flaming tree branch torch wrapped in cloth.

"You will never be forgotten," Hosperan said as he lifted a necklace from around his friend's neck. "May your soul find peace in the life that follows, friend." He touched the torch to the cloth and it caught fire immediately. With the stranger's help, they pushed the raft out to the open water.

Tears flowed from Hosperan's left eye as he watched the flame grow and consume the raft. When the fire had nothing left to burn it was swallowed by the surrounding water. The man's voice ended the ceremony.

"Come, eat," he said.

13

Hosperan closed his eye and took a deep breath.

Then he turned and walked back to the camp and sat on a log and began to eat the meat.

"Lynx meat is pretty good, yes?"

Hosperan didn't respond. He was torn over the fact that he was eating the dead animal that had eaten his friend. He thought it to be some form of vengeance. It also felt quite unethical. But he was hungry. He imagined it to be one of the lynx that he had killed himself.

"I understand," the stranger said as he added another log to the fire. "No need for speaking. You have been through a lot. We will camp together tonight, in case the pack returns. In the morning, we will go our own way."

"What happened to my eye?" Hosperan asked the man.

The stranger paused for a second. It looked like he was trying to find the words. "Your eye is gone. They took it."

"What?"

"After I finished handling the remaining lynx, I checked your friend first. He was beat up pretty bad, as you saw. He wasn't breathing. So, I came over to check on you. You were unconscious, but you still had breath. You had lost a lot of blood. I washed the blood from your face. Once it was clean, there was only a bloody hole where your right eye was supposed to be. I took some medicine from my pack and washed it out to keep it from getting infected and then I bandaged it and put the patch over."

Hosperan couldn't believe what he was hearing. He would never see with both eyes again.

"I did the best I could," the man continued. "You'll probably want to see an actual medicine man when you get wherever you're going."

"I don't understand. This is so much," Hosperan said without looking up. "How did you even find us?"

"Just lucky I guess," the man returned to his log. "I am just passing through, on my way up the mountain. I saw tracks in the snow. Human and animal. I decided to follow the human track in order find whoever was up here before they found me. Once I heard the growling and yells I came as quick as I could."

"Why?"

"I don't know. When I see someone in trouble, I'm not very good at keeping out of it."

"Hmmph," Hosperan grunted.

"What about you boys? What are you doing up here at this time of year?"

"We were heading to the memorial grounds. But it seems pointless now. I am just going to head home in the morning." Hosperan had not taken his eyes off of the fjord since he finished his meal.

"Huh, that's interesting."

"What?"

"That's where I'm heading myself."

"Really?"

"Yeah, to honor the cleansed, of course. Same reason you are, I bet?"

"Something like that."

"Fair enough, you don't have to tell me anything. I'll probably be gone before you wake up in the morning. Good luck on your journey, wherever you decide to go."

Hosperan didn't say anything. He was not sure how to respond. He could not think about anything other than Gildor.

The stranger got up and took off his wet outer and inner top layers and hung them on a branch near the fire. Hosperan caught a glimpse of the shirtless man standing near the flames and saw something that would keep him awake the entire night.

The stranger's entire arm was scarred from what looked like a massive burn wound.

14

Hosperan felt his blood rushing through his veins at an increased speed. He sat up and stared directly at the man. It took the stranger a moment to realize he was being examined. When he finally noticed the eye locked on him, he spoke up.

"Some people say it looks like the skin of the fire beast. I don't really think so. Most people haven't seen the beast up close."

Hosperan still couldn't speak.

No.

It couldn't be.

Hosperan knew what he had to do, but he couldn't find the words. His mind was racing and his mouth could not catch up. After an infinity in front of the fire, Hosperan finally said, "What is your name?"

"I guess we're past the stranger phase. I mean we fought together, buried a friend, shared a meal, and here I am standing half naked," the man laughed a bit at the last part. Hosperan was silent; hanging on every word. Waiting for the name. Waiting for this stranger to wake him from this dream. But it wasn't a dream at all.

It was better than a dream.

"The name's Raknar, yours?"

Hosperan exploded into tears.

"No, it can't be. It can't be. What is this?"

"Kid, calm down. What's wrong with you."

"You have a son, don't you?" Hosperan said as he stood up. Tears rolled off his face and into the dirt. "But you don't know him anymore, right?"

The man leaned back. From the look on his face, it appeared he was going through the same series of emotions Hosperan had just experienced. Nothing outside of the fire's glow mattered in that moment.

"How do you...no. No. Really?" the man said as he walked toward Hosperan and put his hands on the child's shoulders. The child began to speak.

"My name is..."

"Hosperan," his father interrupted.

Now the tears were flowing from every eye in the cleft. Hosperan had dreamed of this moment time and time again. Sometimes he imagined he would be angry with his father and that he would storm away. But that could not be farther from reality.

He melted into his father's arms. His father's real arms. He was embracing his real father. His head was really against his father's chest. And his real father was embracing him. Hosperan lost control of all emotions again as a second realization washed over him.

The father kissed the forehead of his son.

"I'm sure you have more than a few questions," Raknar said as he loosed the embrace of his son. "Where would you like to begin?"

"I don't even," Hosperan began to speak and they sat back down around the fire. "How are you alive?"

"Oh, starting with the easy ones, huh?" his father said. Raknar grabbed another log and placed it over the fire before returning to his seat. "I'm sure you've heard the story about the barrel and the luring the beast away from the village."

"Yeah, and your body was never found. But the barrel was charred."

"Right, well, as soon as the fire beast cleared the village it lost interest in my barrel banging and flew northward. I waited for a while to see if it would return. But it never did. It was actually gone."

"But, why?" Hosperan whispered.

"Ah, yes. Now to the tough questions. While I was waiting, I had time to think. I always thought differently about the fire beast than the rest of the village, but I could never do anything about it or even talk to anyone about it." Hosperan's father turned from looking at his son to looking into the fire. "I decided to fake my death and start over. I burned the barrel myself and sent it down the river. Then I traveled a few days to the north where I came across Hofn. That is where I've been living ever since."

Hosperan's joy was turning into anger. His father had only been a few days journey away from him this entire time? It had to be some kind of joke.

"Why? What have you been doing all these years? Didn't you remember that you had a small child who was now without a father? That you had a son who never had a father to teach him the things of men, like poetry and responsibility. Didn't you think about that?"

"Every day," his father said.

"Then why? Why not come home?"

"It's...complicated. I'll show you the main reason soon. But I'll be honest with you, Son," his father wiped a few tears from his own eyes. "After I had been in Hofn for a few days, word began to spread of my heroics and my sacrifice. All the way from our village to the eastern bank, people were talking about me."

"Yes, you're a legend," Hosperan added.

"Exactly. People thought me greater in death than in life. I couldn't live up to it. I knew you would be in line to be chief and I prayed the eldership to take care of you and your mother. You both were set. But if I were to return, the truth would destroy my legacy. I would be accused of abandonment of chiefly responsibilities and would be sentenced to death. And rightly so. And they would remove you and your mother from power. I couldn't do that."

The anger dissolved. Hosperan began to realize that his father's decision was not as selfish as he first thought. Hosperan stayed silent for a while and processed his thoughts. His father did not bother him.

"Are you really traveling to the memorial grounds?" Hosperan asked.

"Yes, well I was. I don't think it necessary anymore. See, I've been having these dreams where I'm forced to relive the Night of Fire over and over again. And every time it ends with me holding a burning child in my arms. And the child is always saying 'honor me' over and over again," Raknar looked at his son. "And that child is always you."

Hosperan couldn't believe it. His mouth was open like he was about to speak, but nothing came out. His father continued.

"I thought I was honoring you with my work, but, obviously, my soul was not satisfied. So, I thought I would come to the memorial ground to try and figure out how to honor you. There is some kind of special revelation that comes from looking at your own tombstone."

"Unbelievable," Hosperan said.

"I know it sounds strange. And morbid. The dreams of you being on fire and everything. But dreams are dreams. I'm not sure how to control them."

"No, it's not that. That is why I am here as well."

"What do you mean?"

"I've been having dreams, reliving the Night of Fire over and over as well. But it's not me on fire, it's you. And you're holding me up, asking me to honor you. And, of course, I have no idea how to honor a legend. A legend that was sacrificed for me to live. So, I asked my friend what to do and he said when he didn't know what to do, he tried to figure out what his parents would do. They both died in the Night of Fire. The same as you. Well…" Hosperan paused.

"Go on," his father said.

"I thought this to be excellent advice, except that I didn't know enough about you to know what you would do in a given situation. So, I talked to the storyteller and asked him to tell me about you."

"Ah, Krojin is still alive? Bless that man."

"Krojin?"

"That is the storyteller's real name. I know everyone calls him storyteller, but we were friends before he was the storyteller. Anyway, keep going."

"Well, he gave me the advice to visit the memorial grounds in order to honor you. So here I am."

"That is fascinating," his father stood and began to pace. "We are having the same dreams. Well, we were having the same dreams. I doubt they will continue now. This is truly incredible."

"But why?" Hosperan asked. "Why share a dream? What does it mean?"

"I don't know for sure, but I have a good idea. I'll need to show you something. Will you come with me to see my village? To Hofn?"

"How far is it?"

"Only a three day journey. It's just to the north of here."

"I can't. I can't leave my mother for that long. What if the beast comes while I am away."

"Reehna, how is she?"

"She is consumed with the prophecy and only wants me to be chief so she can stay in power. She needs me."

"I'm sorry to hear that. I love your mother dearly. And I've never found another love. But I need you to come with me."

"I cannot leave her like you left us."

Hosperan's words echoed off the wall of the cleft and slowly across the water. No one said anything. The words were still hanging around them.

"Son, let me show you why I left. Come with me. Do you think these dreams will stop if you return home now?" Hosperan didn't answer. He knew they would not stop. He knew he had to go with his father, although his conscience said no.

"We'll leave at first light. And we'll need to make it in two days," Hosperan said in a chief's voice.

"Very well," his father replied.

"Goodnight," Hosperan said as he laid down with his back to the fire and his father.

"Goodnight, Son."

15

The sunrise came early the next morning. Hosperan struggled to wake up. There was a part of him that expected his father to be gone when the morning came. He played this scenario out in his head. He would wake up and curse his father and then make his way back home. The desire for reckoning would be gone. His father would be forgotten. But when Hosperan woke up, a different scenario was unfolding.

"You like fish, right?" said his father.

"Yeah, of course," Hosperan replied. "Thanks."

"No problem. You need some good energy food. You had a long day yesterday, and we've got a long one ahead of us today. You're still recovering. How's your eye?"

"It hurts. But it hurts less than yesterday, so that's something."

"That is something. When we get to Hofn, we'll make sure you see our healer. He'll get it cleaned up and we'll get you a better patch."

"I hadn't considered that. I'm going to have to wear a patch forever."

"I mean, you don't have to necessarily. You just might scare children and most adults away with the open hole on your face. But, up to you."

"I think I'll stick with the patch."

"Good choice," Raknar said as he stood and began to gather his possessions. "Are you about ready to go, Hosperan?"

"I think so," his son replied. He was looking out over the water like he was waiting for someone to walk out of it.

"He fought valiantly, and you have honored him greatly," his father said as he placed his hand on Hosperan's shoulder.

"But I still miss him. I'm still upset."

"As you should be. That's an appropriate response. If you weren't upset, I'd be worried."

"He was my greatest friend. My only friend, really. I just can't believe it."

"I know, Son. I'm sorry. But we need to get moving if we are going to make a three day journey in two. We can let our bodies travel while our souls grieve."

Hosperan didn't say anything. He waited a moment longer before gathering his pack and walking away from the fire, the cleft, and the last place he saw his friend.

They headed north. Hosperan had never been this far north before. All the trade routes went south and east. The raiding ships always went south. It was too cold past Mount Kondor. The harsh conditions made everything die. Maybe that is why his father lived there.

His father led the way, but he never got too far ahead. Hosperan could see his father checking over his shoulder after every few steps. They walked back down the path Hosperan and his friend had traveled a lifetime before; no, the morning before. They veered off of the familiar trail before the snow turned to dirt and headed down the north side of Mount Kondor. His father traveled with an axe in hand, and Hosperan with his spear that doubled as a walking stick. He used it to support his weight and to supplement his vision on his right side.

"Make sure you're drinking enough water. It'll help you heal and keep your strength," his father said.

"I know," Hosperan replied. His father changed the subject quickly. "Your birthday is coming up, huh. That's exciting."

"For who?"

"Usually the person having the birthday. You know, the one being celebrated. I know they celebrate birthdays in Kilbo."

"My birthday has always been a joke. It's not about me. It's always 'seven more years until you're chief' or 'only two more years.' It's not celebrating me. It's just a milestone on the road to chiefdom. And every year I grow less excited because that means I am that much closer to being a man. That much closer to being chief."

"Do you not care to be the chief?"

"I don't know. It hardly means anything. The elders still make the decisions. I can't do anything. No one can."

"That's not true," his father replied. "I wasn't born into the royal family, you know. I was a farmer who built places to store my crops. I loved building these structures. I experimented with all kinds of wood and different ways to hold them together. Then I tried a mixture of wood and stone. And then all stone. The village was impressed. The chief especially. He asked me to build him a home from stone. So I got to work."

"Why are you telling me this?" Hosperan interrupted.

"Because I built these homes with a strong center hold. You know why?"

"No."

"To protect people from the fire beast. I knew that after I built the chief's home, other people would ask me to build them one too. My plan was to build the strong center room and then convince everyone to go there to pray during the Night of Fire.

But it turned out that the chief and his entire family died during that Night of Fire, before I had their home complete. I was elected as chief not long after. Then I just ordered everyone to go to their center hold to pray when the beast arrived."

Hosperan was thinking on all of this, but he still did not put it together. They had reached the bottom of the mountain and were now walking side by side through a field.

"Don't you see? I wanted to save the villagers from the fire beast. And I did. Sacrifices during the Night of Fire decreased drastically since the new houses were built. You see, I found a way to make a difference, to help people. I didn't need to wait to come to power to do it. That's the mindset necessary to make a good group of people great. That is the mindset in Hofn. Everyone trying to help everyone. It's beautiful."

"But, why would you want to save people from being sacrificed? Is that right?"

"That is a great question, Son. And one that will be answered when we arrive. For now, just know that I have found a new sense of peace in these last ten years. A new sense of purpose."

"It's more important than your purpose of being a father? A husband?" Hosperan questioned.

"It's because I want to be a great father and husband and chief and neighbor and friend and human. It's a purpose that serves all of these desires. It wasn't easy, if that's what you're asking. You'll understand soon enough, Son. Soon enough."

Hosperan was too tired to pry. He was unsure what his father was talking about, but it was obvious that this aged man spoke with great passion and deep conviction. They talked little during the remainder of the trip. Hosperan went to bed early that night and they rose early the next morning. There was only small talk between them.

Hosperan had begun to worry about his mother. If there was any trouble, she was now at least three days away. He doubted his decision to join his father. He doubted his decision to go to the memorial grounds. He doubted his decision to leave the village.

But all of this was forgotten late on that second day when he heard his father speak.

"We're here."

16

They had walked to the top of a hill when the arrangement of stone houses became visible. The sun was setting to their left. A few homes had light glowing from their windows. Farmers were leaving their fields. People were walking around in the streets. A man led a horse to the front of a house, and tied it to a pole. A mother was calling for her children to come inside. Everyone acknowledged Hosperan's father as they passed.

"Hey Raknar, welcome back," said the man with the horse.

"Hi Jorn. How's Lawiin's hoof?"

"She'll be fine. Just need to fill in that ditch north of town. Watch your step."

"Thanks for the heads up," Raknar said. They continued to walk through town.

"Did you bring us anything?" said one of the children as they ran up to Hosperan's father.

"Of course," his father said as he reached in his sack. The children tried to peek so they could be the first one to see the gift. He pulled out multiple strips of fur. "It's the hide of a giant bear. Wear it as a headband long enough and one day you'll be as strong as a bear!"

"Like that guy?" one of the children said as they pointed to the patch covering Hosperan's eye.

"Exactly! This is Hosperan the Bearorka. They call him that because he is strong and mighty, like a bear!"

The children's eyes lit up. Raknar handed them all a headband and told them they better get home before dark. The children scattered and one of the mothers waved to Raknar as the children entered the home.

"We didn't see any bears on our trip," Hosperan asked.

"You weren't with me at the beginning of my trip." Hosperan considered the magnitude of facing a bear and lynx in the span of a few days. It was simply incredible. "But you're right. I ran into a trader after the first day and traded him for the bear pelt."

"But the children?"

"I never said I killed the bear. I just said it would give them strength. And it will. Hopefully when they need it most. Does it matter where that strength comes from if it helps them push through a difficult time?"

"I don't know. It just seems wrong."

"Maybe it is? Who am I to judge," his father said. They arrived at a house with a small door. Raknar knocked and said, "Tondl, it's Raknar. It's an emergency."

Moments later the door opened and a man half of Hosperan's size stood behind it.

"Everything is an emergency with you, Raknar," said the old man. He laughed a howling laugh that echoed through the house. "What can I do for you and your?"

"Son," Raknar answered.

"Well then, come in, Son," Tondl said.

The medicine man didn't ask any other questions during their visit. It was as if the medicine man had known Hosperan his entire life. The man called Hosperan by name and gave his condolences for the loss of his friend.

Then the man removed the eye patch in order to clean the wound. He sprinkled some kind of powder directly in Hosperan's eye hole. The powder spilled onto most of his face. Then he told Hosperan not to wash until sunrise. He recommended rabbit pelts for new eye patches. He said they are the most durable. After that they thanked the man and left his house. The streets were empty by this time.

"Now what?" Hosperan asked.

"Now we go home. It is just up the street," Raknar said as he pointed. "We need to get you in bed before the powder hardens. And, I'm ready to sleep in my own bed."

When Raknar said his house was just up the street, he meant they would follow this road until it led out of town half a mile. Raknar led the way as they traveled by torchlight. Hosperan felt light on his feet and a bit disoriented after they left the medicine man's house. He was having trouble walking straight.

"Looks like the healing powder is starting to kick in," Raknar said.

"What's happening? I can barely walk," Hosperan replied. "The trees are talking to me. Do you hear that? What do you want trees?"

"I forgot to mention that the powder is incredible for healing wounds, but it has hallucinogenic side effects," his father said laughing. "They should wear off in the morning."

"My toes just decided they don't want to be part of my feet anymore. No, toes! Please. Don't leave. I need you. I need you," Hosperan said as he bent down and began running his hand over the front of his feet.

"Okay, Son. We need to get you in bed. Come on, almost there."

Hosperan felt his arm move involuntarily and then wrap itself around his father's shoulder. They began to walk. A small building appeared. It was halfway underground. The roof was the top of a hill with grass covering it.

"Are you a rabbit?" Hosperan asked. "You live in a burrow like a rabbit, but you barely look like a rabbit."

His father just laughed as he shut the door behind them. Hosperan couldn't believe how big his father's home was on the inside compared to the outside. It was massive. Bigger than the great hall where the elders meet. Hosperan couldn't even see where the room ended because the light from the torch did not reach that far. There were wooden poles stretching from the floor to the ceiling located every couple of feet. This proved quite difficult for Hosperan to navigate with one eye and with whatever medicine he was given.

On his way through the wooden maze, he did notice the home was scarcely decorated, save a few maps and weapon racks. The maps had handwriting and drawings all over. Books were scattered across multiple tables and the floor. Hosperan felt uncomfortable in the room. He was sure the medicine was making him crazy.

His father lit a large candle next to a small bed. Hosperan discarded most of his layers and got under the covers. His father went farther back into the room. After a moment, Hosperan rolled onto his left shoulder and faced the front door where they had just entered. There was a large pelt hanging on the wall next to the door that Hosperan had missed when they first entered. It had three words written on it.

"What does 'When embers end' mean?" Hosperan asked as he struggled to keep his eye open.

Raknar walked back into the room and kneeled next to Hosperan. He kissed his son's forehead and whispered, "Let's save that one for tomorrow. Goodnight, Son."

17

Hosperan woke and his face was stiff. He could not open his eye or move his jaw. His only breathing passed through his nose. This was no issue while he slept since his relaxed body was able to manage the small amount of air intake. But, now that he was conscious, he became anxious. He sat up and began tearing off the hardened powder. The mask had started to grow into his skin. He was able to remove the layer from the bottom of his face first. His mouth was exposed and he gasped for air.

"I didn't know if you were going to make it," he heard a voice from across the room.

"What's happening. What is this stuff?" Hosperan replied.

"It's the healing powder from last night. It hardens over time. But that's how it heals. You remember going to the medicine man, right?"

"Yeah, I remember that. But I don't remember how I got here," Hosperan said, as he peeled the last part of the mask off and steadied his breathing. "I actually don't even know where 'here' is. Is this where you live?"

"You got it," his father replied.

"It's so massive. And warm. How is it so warm?"

"Well, we're mostly underground. This home is built into the side of a hill. So, the Earth around us helps keep the heat from our bodies inside. Pretty cool, huh?"

"I've never seen anything like this. Could you go deeper into the earth?"

"Certainly. I thought it would be incredible to have a home that looks like a cattle shack from the outside…"

"But be a massive castle on the inside."

"Exactly," his father said with a smile.

"That's cool," Hosperan said. He was out of bed by now and was examining the floor and ceiling. "The ground above must put great strain on the ceiling. Is that why there are so many pillars inside?"

"That's right. I haven't found a better way to distribute the weight. So, I have to settle for poles every couple of feet. A small price to pay."

"Worth it," Hosperan said. His focus began to shift from the material of the walls to the material on the walls. Now that he was looking around, he remembered seeing the maps and the weapons from the night before.

"Why have you drawn on all of these maps? Are they inaccurate?" Hosperan asked.

"I hope not. I'm betting my life on them being right."

Hosperan's father was sitting in a chair and motioned for his son to join him. Steam rose from cooked vegetables on the table between the chairs. Hosperan sat down and began to eat.

"These maps account for the entire world. Some of them are duplicates and some are parts that I've had to hand draw. They were inaccurate or incomplete."

"But why? Are you planning a trip?"

"In a way, yes," his father said. Then he stood and ran his finger along the drawn line of the map.

"You see these lines? These represent a path."

"New roads? For better trade?"

"No, Son. This is the path of the fire beast." Hosperan was silent. He gathered his thoughts and was about to speak, but his father began again. "Well, it's our best guess at the path the beast takes on its journey across the world."

"This is great. So, everyone can have time to prepare themselves for the ritual; for when the beast arrives."

"Not exactly, Hosperan," his father sat back in the chair and looked directly into his son's face. "The beast is not of this world. It is evil. Pure evil."

Hosperan was surprised by his father's blatant heresy. He had similar thoughts as his father, sure, but no one spoke like this. It caught Hosperan off-guard.

"I can't just sit by and let the destruction and death keep happening over and over." His father pointed to a different part of the map. "You see this blank spot to the left? The fire beast is untraceable when he goes to the west."

"What does it do? What is there?"

"I don't know. But, during its journey, it spends four years across the sea before returning. You know what I think? I think that is where it lives. Its home is there. I don't know yet."

"Yet? What do you mean?" Hosperan asked. "You don't mean that you are going west. To cross the sea? That alone is madness. But to do so in search of the fire beast. Unthinkable." Raknar said nothing. He let his son talk it out. "What do you plan to do when you get there? And how are you going to get enough people to curse the gods and follow you? You need a ship and a crew, cooks, tradesmen, and....warriors." Hosperan was pacing in front of the map. He realized what he was doing and sat back down. "What are you going to do if you make it there?"

"You asked me last night what this saying means, what 'When embers end' means. It's more than just words. It's a symbol. It's a promise. All the people you met, and all the ones who live here that you have yet to meet, they all fly this flag. We are all united under it. It gives us hope for our grandchildren and it brings us closer to the gods.

We stand behind this symbol knowing we can shift the course of history for the better. You see, it is more than just words, it is how we align our lives." Raknar was standing now, staring at the words. Hosperan could only see his father's back, but he did see him wipe something from his eyes. "Son, this is the reason I had to leave you. I hope you will understand. Because these three words will change everything."

"It's just so much. Those three words inspire you?" Hosperan asked.

"The full saying is 'We burn brightest...when embers end,'" his father replied. "It means humanity will be its truest self when the flames from the fire beast are no more." Hosperan took a moment to consider what his father was saying. After he gathered his thoughts, he replied.

"You're going to kill the fire beast?" Hosperan asked.

"Yes," his father replied. "But not just me. Everyone in this village is with me."

"What about tradition? We've been taught the fire beast does the work of the gods."

"Well, we've heard there is a book older than any of the traditions we have here. We've heard it tells the true story of how we came to be. The true story of the fire beast."

"But you've never read it yourself?" Hosperan asked.

"Not yet. It's believed to be in the west," his father replied.

"So, you're going to kill the fire beast and find this book?"

"That's right."

"But what about everyone in Kilbo? They all think you are dead. They all think you're a legend. This isn't right. You need to tell them the truth. Come back with me."

"Son, you know I can't do that."

"How can you not? You're living a lie here."

"If I go back I will be labeled a shameful svikr and you and your mother will be pulled from power. You won't be chief and your mother will be forced to work the mill. And I'll probably be killed on the spot for death fraud. Is that what you want, Son?"

Hosperan didn't speak. He never considered the weight of truth. He wrestled with the consequences of suffering for the truth or benefitting from a lie.

"Of course not," he finally said. "It just doesn't seem right."

"I know, Son. I can't tell you how many nights I've sat in this house and wrestled with myself over whether or not I should return to you. I weighed every option. Every positive and negative consequence."

"And I lost," Hosperan said.

"No, the future of humanity won." His father leaned forward and put his hands on Hosperan's knees. "When we kill that beast, we will keep it from killing thousands, if not millions, of people in the years to come. They will not have to fear the flames engulfing their homes and melting the flesh off their loved ones in front of them, only to have their home collapse while they are inside praying. It is a sacrifice for a brighter future. I knew you could bear the burden of not having me there, and look at you. You've become an incredible man." Tears began to fall from both of their faces.

"What about the gods?" Hosperan asked. "We've been taught that if the beast takes our bodies, it's because we're a sacrifice to the gods. If you kill the beast, you're killing the gods' messenger."

"But, think about this. The gods took a part of themselves and made us, right?" his father replied.

"Yeah."

"Then why would they want to kill us? Why would they want to kill their creation? Why would they want to kill a part of themselves? Do you know why we were created?"

"To honor the gods, right?"

"Exactly. And rightfully so," his father sat back in his chair. "So, if the gods took a piece of themselves to create us to worship them, why would they send a beast to kill us? That just leaves less people to give them worship. It doesn't add up."

"What are you saying?" Hosperan asked.

"I'm saying our ancestors made up the myth that the beast cleanses. It's a primitive coping mechanism. They couldn't deal with the fact that their gods would let something so destructive exist, so it was either deny the gods or include the fire beast."

"And you think this is all in that book in the west?"

"I know it."

"Well, you can't know it. You've never read it."

"Even if I read it, it doesn't mean I know it. It's bigger than that."

Hosperan didn't respond. He stared at WHEN EMBERS END written on the pelt. His father's words swirled around his head. He couldn't completely deny what his father was saying. It made sense logically and he was beginning to have these same thoughts, he just didn't have the words for them.

He thought back to when he shared these thoughts with Gildor on their last night. His friend had stuck by him even though Hosperan spoke of radical things. But Hosperan began to realize the difference in talking about something radical, and actually doing something radical. It is much different to see it in action; and a complete jolt to partake in the change.

"Let's go for a walk," his father said. As they left the home in the hill, his father began speaking again, but this time in a much gentler tone. "What do you see, Hosperan?" his father said as they neared the town.

"A village? I don't know. It looks just like our...I mean, my village."

"Exactly. These people are not raging savages or incessant radicals. They are just regular people who saw something wrong in the world and decided to take action."

As they walked the streets, there were teenagers sitting on benches listening to a man teach them about seafaring. There were men and women taking turns aiming their bows at targets. There was a blacksmith molding swords and small blades. A group of children were hauling crops into a storage container.

Hosperan never thought anything unusual about the village when he first encountered it. And he didn't consider the village abnormal now either. They are just people.

"I need to be alone for a while. Please don't follow me. I know my way back to the house."

"Of course, Son. Whatever you wish."

Hosperan made his way south on the path he and his father had traveled the night before. The path toward Kilbo.

18

It did not take long for Hosperan to descend down the sloping path. The village was blocked by the hill. He was alone.

The night before, he had seen a clearing on the mountain wall beside them that looked as if it ascended up the mountain. A rock ice cliff stuck itself out overlooking the river. This is where Hosperan wanted to go.

He made his way into the clearing, which he discovered was not a clearing at all. The rocks and plants were just smaller. The only weapon he had with him was his dagger. He pulled it from the sheath around his waist and began clearing the frozen plants. The sun shown on the mountainside and reflected off the snow causing him to squint as he made his way.

The path proved to be longer than he originally assumed and the plant life much more resilient. The reflected light began to dim as the sun reached its dusk. But Hosperan was not concerned with any of these things. All he could think about were his dreams.

"Honor me, honor me. Honor you how? By joining your apostate army?" Hosperan said these things as he hacked away at the overgrowth. "I just had thoughts of rebellion. Nothing like this. This is crazy."

Just then he came to a clearing. The path led out to the overhang. He walked with reverence across the rock bridge until he came to the end. He was immersed in his surroundings. He could see the ocean to the west. The coastline stretched in both directions. The sun was sinking into the water which colored the sky with temporary brilliance.

"How could the gods create something so beautiful and yet send an evil beast to do something so detestable? It doesn't make sense. And yet here I am questioning my father's plans."

Hosperan sat with his feet hanging over the edge of the path. The river cut through the trees below him. His father's village was visible if he looked behind him. They were having a fire.

He looked to his left, to the south. He thought he could see a glint of light coming from that direction. He believed it to be his village. It didn't mean much anymore. His friend was no longer there. The myth surrounding his father was a hollow pillar holding up their society. His mother was power mad. And he believed his cousin was conspiring with the elders to have him killed.

"Please stop the dreams," Hosperan yelled to the ether. "I don't even know what honor is anymore."

The moon had taken over as the provider of light. Hosperan sat still. In his mind, there was a battle raging between honesty and truth, fear and courage, tradition and logic, word and action, respect and honor.

"I can't take it anymore! I don't know what you want," he said to all the invisible gods at once. "I need a sign. Help me. Please. I've only asked for help once before. Please." Hosperan stood to his feet and looked over the edge of the cliff.

"I'm going to jump off this cliff into the river. If I die, so be it. I will be forgotten like those before me. Neither my father or mother will miss me. He abandoned me and she is only using me." Hosperan lowered his voice and closed his eye. "But if I live, I'll know it's because you have spared me so I can join my father in his quest. I commit myself to your will."

And with that prayer, Hosperan jumped from the cliff.

19

The draft created by Hosperan's falling body forced the eye covering off his head. The sound of moving water grew in intensity until he broke the threshold between air and liquid.

He figured he would have hit a jagged rock or the riverbed immediately, but neither of those things happened. He went as deep as his momentum would take him and then started floating toward the surface.

He floated to the top and took a breath. The jagged rock cliff where he had just gambled with his life was shrinking out of view as the river carried him toward the sea.

He was alive.

The gods had spoken.

His old life was now a memory. He was to join his father's cause and fight the beast. His mind was as crisp as the air surrounding him. It was time to tell his father the news.

The current flowed like a stoic. Hosperan had no trouble making his way toward the bank. The only problem he faced was his soaking wet clothes. It was cold enough that a light snow had begun to fall. He knew he needed to get to his father's house fast or his revelation would be short lived.

Hosperan ran undignified through the forest. Tears of joy freezing to his smile-stained face. The path to the village had become familiar to him and it did not take long to find it. There were a few people still outside as he came to the top of the hill and walked into the village. They were talking and sitting around their fires. When Hosperan came into view, they stopped talking. One man called out to him.

"Do you need some help, boy?" said a man adding a log to the fire.

"No sir, I just need to find Raknar."

"Raknar? What do you need with him?" Then the man spoke again without giving Hosperan a chance to answer. "You're soaking wet, come over by the fire before you freeze to death."

"I can't do that, sir. I need to find my father."

"Your father?" the man stood up. "Raknar is your father?"

"Yes sir."

"Well, my goodness. You must be new around here. Have you come to join our fight against the fire beast?"

Hosperan paused for a moment. This would be the first time he publicly acknowledged his heresy. There would be no going back. The decision had been made in his heart, but he was not sure it had completely resonated in his brain. He was planning to kill the beast.

It took him a few extra moments to respond, but then the words came to him. He put his hand on the man's shoulders and looked directly into his eyes and said, "When embers end."

20

"Ah ha!" the man bellowed. "This boy! Excellent! Welcome." The man took off his outer layer and wrapped it around Hosperan. The immediate change of temperature was astounding. Hosperan didn't realize he was literally beginning to freeze.

"Thank you, sir," Hosperan replied to the gesture.

"Of course. We owe Raknar very much. Do you need help finding your way?"

"No sir, I think I know how to find his rabbit hole from here."

"Ha! And a sense of humor. This boy is great! Let us know if you need anything else."

"Thank you."

Hosperan turned his back toward the fire and made his way to the house in the hill. He could hear the group begin to sing some kind of song. It sounded like a victory song to Hosperan. His heart was warmed; both because of the acceptance into this community and because of the new coat draped over him.

It did not take long for him to find his father's door. He reached his hand up to the door to knock, but paused. This was the moment his dreams had been leading him toward. Now he hoped to not let his father down. Before he could knock the door opened.

"Son? You're soaking wet. Come in here." The warmth of the insulated underground home consumed him as he walked in and began to take off his wet clothes. His father grabbed some of his own clothes and brought them to his son. Hosperan sat in his chair, now in dry clothes, with a blanket wrapped around him.

"What happened, Son?"

"You might not believe it all, but I believe you'll be pleased with the outcome."

"Well, go on then. You can't build it up like that and then leave an old man hanging." Hosperan sat back in his chair to get comfortable and his father leaned forward on his. Then Hosperan began to tell him what happened.

"After I left the house, I went to a place I had seen when we arrived in the village last night. A place where a rock bridge overlooks the river."

"Ah yes, Jonnil Peak. The bridge to the gods."

"What?"

"They say the bridge continues into the gods' realm and is one of the places the gods use to enter into our world. People say they've seen a circle of swirling light up there. Why?"

"Well, once I reached the peak I could see everything. It was stunning. And it made me think about this land. About my home village and Mother and Gildor and the dreams and the beast and the gods and the heresy and you. I asked the gods for clarity. I asked for direction. I asked for a sign."

"And," his father said, hanging on every word.

"I said, 'If I jump off this bridge and die, so be it. I'll be forgotten like those before me. But if I jump off this bridge and live, then I'll take that as a sign that the gods have spared my life in order to join my father and kill the beast.'" Hosperan could see the tears falling from his father's eyes. "And then I jumped."

"Son," his father cried.

"I know. Foolish. But here I am. I hit the icy water and was saved from dashing into the rocks or riverbed. Then I swam to shore and made my way back here."

"The gods provide. My goodness." His father sat back in his seat and put his hands on his face. Hosperan used the blanket to wipe his own tears. Then his father spoke again.

"But the coat? Where did you get this pelt?"

"When I entered the village, I was stopped by some people sitting around a fire. A large man stopped me. He had long hair and a serpent tattoo on his neck. After I told him who I was and what I was here to do, he welcomed me and gave me his coat."

"Ah, Shryonell. That old man. What a guy. A great warrior, but better leader."

"I think I would have frozen to death if it wasn't for his kindness. I didn't even realize that I couldn't feel my legs or arms."

"Saved by the gods and saved by man. Looks like they are working together to make sure you made it back here."

"I think you're right. When I came up out of the water, I had a sense of clarity. My mind was at peace. And I knew what I had to do." Hosperan sat up and looked into his father's eyes, "What we have to do."

His father wept again and reached out his hand and Hosperan grabbed it and held on tight. It did not take long for the hand hug to turn into a body hug. After a few moments, Hosperan grabbed his father's hand again and whispered, "When embers end"

With tears in his eyes, his father replied, "When embers end, indeed."

21

Hosperan slept well that evening. He had no dreams. He woke warm and ready to make a difference.

"So, what do we do first? Some kind of training or strategy meeting?" Hosperan said as he ate his breakfast.

"Well, that all depends on what you want to do. Everyone has a different part to play. We all can't be archers, or we wouldn't have anyone to navigate the ship. And we can't all be tacticians, or we wouldn't have anyone to fight."

Hosperan was a bit embarrassed by his lack of knowledge, but he swallowed it between bites of rabbit. "We've had the luxury of time," his father continued. "According to our maps and speaking with other villages, we believe the beast attacks this coast last before making the trip to his homeland across the sea. We have had time to prepare. We have had time to let everyone discover their strengths and let them figure out how to use them for the cause."

"Does that work? Do you have enough people distributed among the needs?"

"Unfortunately, no. We're lacking skilled warriors, of course. The village decided long ago that battle skills will be the secondary skill for most. Everyone is required to have basic battle training, in case they are needed. But their main skill is where they spend most of their focus."

"That makes sense. Why have a giant army if you don't have the sailors and the cooks and the blacksmiths and the healers required to get the warriors into battle."

"That's right. Once the battle begins, anyone can become a competent soldier," his father said as he looked at his maps.

"When are you…I mean, we leaving? To go west?" Hosperan asked.

"Soon. After the beast attacks, we'll see if it flees west. If he does, then we'll ready our ships and follow behind."

"Woah, so you mean soon soon. Like, as soon as tomorrow soon."

"It could be today," his father replied. "The ships are stocked and hidden in a cove up the coast.'"

"Incredible," Hosperan replied. "But why not go now? Why not get a head start and beat the beast to its homeland?"

"It was considered. We just finished preparations and we didn't want to be in open sea while the beast is making its trip home. An encounter with the beast at sea would put us at a tremendous disadvantage. We want to make sure the beast is out in front of us so that we can surprise it."

"Hmm," Hosperan grunted.

"Maybe the other reason for our delay was so that you could join us. Perhaps we need your skills.

Whatever they may be. I know you have some battle skills. You survived an attack from a pack of lynx."

"All I do is train. Unfortunately, the result of that battle was not favorable."

"Well, you were without a weapon. To survive hand to hand combat with a pack of lynx is a major feat in itself. You did all you could do." His father went to the wall where multiple weapons were displayed. "What is your weapon of choice, Son?"

"I love the spear," Hosperan answered. "But I don't know if I lost my ability when I lost my eye."

His father grabbed a few spears from the wall and moved to the door. "Well, let's go find out."

...

They walked even farther north on the road surrounded by trees until they came to a clearing. The field was similar to Hosperan's training ground at home, except this field was twice as large and the grass was neatly trimmed all around. Back home, Hosperan mainly practiced with the spear. He liked how he could use it when fighting an enemy in close combat or attack from a distance.

His father went and stood by a stack of hay along the tree line near where they entered.

"Will you help me with this?" his father said as he pointed toward the haystacks.

"With what?"

"We need to take the front layer off."

"I thought we were going to do some weapon training?"

"We are."

Raknar began pulling hay bales off the stack and tossing them to the side. Hosperan didn't know what else to do, so he climbed up the stack and joined his father in pulling bales off. After they had moved the top few layers, Hosperan figured it out.

"You've hidden weapons in here."

"You got it."

"What's all in here?"

"Bows, arrows, swords, axes, spears, shields. You name it, it's probably here."

"Seems pretty risky, to keep all of these weapons just sitting out here."

"Oh, no. Not at all. This is just one collection. And these are mostly for training purposes. We've got weapons hidden all over the city. Not to mention that everyone has their own set."

"So many weapons."

"Remember how I said everyone has a baseline weaponry skill?"

"Yeah."

"Well, that means we need a lot of weapons."

Hosperan nodded with understanding. He didn't consider that everyone in the village was armed and skilled in battle. He wasn't sure if this made him feel safe or in danger. He didn't dwell on it long before changing the subject.

"So, what is your go to weapon?" Hosperan asked.

"Good question," his father said as he surveyed the weapons. "I'm trying to master the majority of the weapons you see here. You never know what you'll be equipped with in battle. But the bow and arrow is my favorite by far." He reached down and picked up a wooden bow and quiver. "I have to admit, I love the showmanship of the bow. It is quite amazing to see someone hit a target at an incredible distance. Also, the stealth is a bonus. And the precision, too."

His father drew the bow and took aim at a sack of hay swinging by a rope from a pole on the other end of the field. After a few seconds, his father released the arrow. It flew toward the target. Seconds later the arrow stuck to the wooden pole holding up the target and the target fell to the ground. Hosperan's father had hit the rope being used to hang the target on the pole.

"Not bad," Hosperan said with a smile.

"Not bad?" his father laughed. "Shall I try left handed?"

"It's a stationary target. The enemy is rarely stationary." Hosperan grabbed a spear from the stack. "And sometimes it attacks when you aren't expecting it." He threw the spear into the air toward the fallen target. Without skipping a beat his father drew his bow once more and took aim. Moments later he released and the arrow knocked the spear off its original course.

"Okay, now I am impressed."

"Wait until you go recover the spear."

Hosperan was intrigued so he jumped off the hay stack and made his way toward the fallen spear. His father walked beside him. They came to the spot where the spear had fallen. Hosperan couldn't believe it.

"Incredible," Hosperan said as he picked up the spear. "You've managed to hit the end of the spear. On the top. It's got to be smaller than a gold coin." Hosperan stood staring at the arrow that was sticking in the end of the wooden spear. "You're going to have to teach me that one."

"Ha, of course, Son." His father pulled the arrow out of the spear and handed the spear back to his son. "Now let's see what you can do. Hit that target straight ahead."

The target was only fifty or sixty paces away. It was hanging on a pole next to the fallen target.

"I should be able to hit this in my sleep. Honestly. I'm not trying to show off anymore."

"You've lost an eye. The way you've maneuvered in the world for almost sixteen years has changed completely. You have to learn things again. Don't beat yourself up too much. Just give it a try."

Hosperan raised the spear to his right ear and took a deep breath. He focused on the target ahead of him and released. The spear flew over the target and into the hay wall behind.

"Unbelievable."

"It might take some time to get the precision back. The good news is that your form is impeccable. You just need to practice."

"We don't have time to practice. I've been practicing my entire life. And now the fire beast could come at any moment and I've got the skills of a child in training school." Hosperan began to walk toward the spear he had just thrown. In his peripherals, he could see his father following close behind. "I need to say goodbye to Mother."

"That's out of nowhere," his father replied. "You need to train out here for a few weeks first."

"There's no time for that. The beast could come at any time. I need to tell her what I've decided to do. About my new path. She deserves to know. You don't have to come. I'll go on my own. Then I'll travel back here and train until it's time to go into battle. But I have to do this. She needs to know."

Hosperan wrapped his hand around the spear. With his head down, he said, "I'm sorry. But I'm going to leave first thing in the morning."

Before he could pull the spear out from the hay, he felt a hand cover his. Then his father spoke.

"I'm coming with you."

22

"But I'm not going to enter the village," his father continued. "If anyone sees me, I'll be killed."

"And so will your legacy." Neither of them said a word. Hosperan could not believe he just spoke out against his father in this way. Hosperan dropped his head.

"Come, let's head back to my house."

They were halfway to the house before anyone spoke again. The conviction Hosperan spoke stuck like a wedge between them. Hosperan tried to find the words to say in order to erase what had been said. He had nothing. He knew his father was upset with him. And then his father spoke.

"You're right, Son. My legacy would be destroyed. And, of course, I like being the subject of great fame." Raknar paused to clear his throat before continuing. "I felt called to kill the fire beast. That's why I left. But the fact that my legend outgrew me is what kept me away. I'm sorry."

"I'm sorry too, Father. I didn't mean it that way. I don't think I meant it like that anyway. And, if you were to come back, then they would have killed you and remove me and Mother from power. You were right."

"It makes my heart glad to hear you say that, Son."

His father reached over and put his arm around his son. They walked like this until they reached the house. Hosperan entered first and his father closed the door behind them.

"So, what's the plan?" his father asked.

"What do you mean?" Hosperan replied.

"Well, you can't just go walking into Kilbo and announce that you have decided to commit your life to making the beast pay for what it has done."

"I guess I don't need to speak to anyone except Mother. Better for everyone to think I died in the mountains on the way to memorial grounds."

"I think that'd be for the best. No need for the other villagers to know you're still alive."

"I could just sneak into the house late one night and speak to Mother then."

"What are you going to say to her?"

"I don't know. I think I'll tell her the truth. She deserves to know. No more lies."

"Of course."

His father put the remaining weaponry back on the wall before walking toward the back of the room.

"I'm going to bed. We've got a long few days ahead of us. We'll leave at first light tomorrow. Good night, son."

"Good night, father."

Hosperan took off his outer layer and his eye patch before getting into bed, but was unable to sleep. His father's question echoed in his mind, "What are you going to say to her?"

He had no idea. How do you tell someone you love that you no longer think about the world the way they do? He knew his mother would not approve. She would think him mad. She would never tell anyone though. She would lose her place of power if the village knew that her son was a shameful svikr.

What if she said, "Why can't you be a wonderful leader like your father?" Would he tell her that her husband was alive? He couldn't. He shouldn't. That was not his secret to tell. He hoped he would be able to take the verbal assault and not have to hurt her with the truth.

How much detail should he share with her about his conversion? How much did she need to know? He would just play it by ear and answer her questions. He knew she would be full of them. All of this hinged on how much time they would have. Hosperan would like to spend as much time as possible with her, but he knew he would be limited. They would need to get back and prepare for departure and continue training.

His training.

He had forgotten how pathetic his display of talent with the spear had been earlier that day. He considered himself a warrior and was unable to complete such a basic maneuver. Although he didn't like it, Hosperan came to the conclusion that he would not be able to stay in Kilbo for long. He desperately needed to come back and train. There would be no use for him in battle if he couldn't wield a weapon. There were so many things on his mind.

His mother.

The truth.

Shameful svikr.

The fire beast.

Honor me.

All these thoughts circled around Hosperan's head as he fell asleep.

23

The scene was familiar.

Kilbo.

There was fire in the street where Hosperan stood. Entire tree branches had caught aflame and had fallen onto houses and into the street. The flames were taller than Hosperan.

Before he knew it, he was standing in front of his house. There were flames escaping from the windows and the roof was slowly caving in. He heard a familiar voice cry out from within the house, "Hosperan! Son, save me."

It was his mother.

As he began to make his way inside the house, the fire lowered and began to dance out of control. The wind picked up and knocked Hosperan off his feet and onto his back. From the dirt road bed, he saw the winged creature descending.

It landed on his house and caused it to collapse. "Mother!" Hosperan cried out.

The beast raised its head above the trees and began to laugh. There was no one else in the village. Hosperan was the only one left who could fight the beast. He pulled out his spear and threw it at the beast.

Too high, miss.

He pulled out another from the quiver on his back. Too high again, miss.

He repeated this over and over. And again, and again he is left with the same result.

Miss after miss after miss.

The fire beast continued to laugh at Hosperan's futile attempts.

Then Hosperan heard the sound of thunder coming from the forest. The beast heard it too. The thunder grew louder and louder until soldiers from his father's village emerge dressed in full battle attire. They were shouting and running toward the beast.

The beast did not stick around for the villagers to come close enough to attack. After three or four flaps of its wings, it ascended and flew west over open water.

Hosperan didn't hesitate to check the rubble where his home once stood. "Mother! Mother!" he cried out as he lifted pieces of charred wood.

His mother was pinned under a couple large pieces of wood. One of them pierced her side. She was barely breathing.

"Mother! No! I'm sorry. I should never have left you here alone. Don't die, Mother. I'm here."

His mother tried to speak but could not. And then without warning her entire arm caught fire. She screamed in pain. The fire spread from her arm until it covered her entire body. Hosperan had to shield his eye from the light of his burning mother.

As he blinked he felt a hot grip on his shoulders. His flaming mother had grabbed ahold of him.

"Mother, please, stop. Let me go. Let me help you. Please."

Moments later she let out a terrifying scream that shook Hosperan to the core. He was not sure what to do. He could not escape her grasp. She was pulling him closer to her.

He was just inches from her face when he heard a whisper through the flames, "Honor me. Honor me."

24

Hosperan sat up out of bed. He was drenched in sweat and was unable to return to sleep. The dream was too disturbing. He got up and started getting ready for the trip home.

"You're up early," his father said as he packed his bag.

"Couldn't sleep, bad dreams," Hosperan replied.

"Aye? Me too. It was strange. Just like the dreams I was having about you before we ran into each other. Except this time, it was your mother saying 'Honor me' instead of you."

"Someone is trying to tell us something."

"What do you mean?"

"My dream was exactly like the dreams I was having before too. Except this time, instead of you, it was Mother saying the same thing. 'Honor me.'" Hosperan put some extra eye patches in his bag and then closed it up. "What do you think it means? Why do you think it's happening?"

"It could be the gods. In fact, I'm sure it is. But why?"

"Maybe trying to tell us to watch out? To beware of the beast?"

"It's possible," his father responded. "It could be some kind of confirmation too. Since we're having the same dreams, it could mean that we're on the same page. Or, that they're telling us that they approve."

"Hmm...I never considered that."

"Maybe it's a sign that our minds and souls are one. That we are on the right path."

"But what about the dreams themselves?" Hosperan asked. "Why does it have to be Mother dying. What does she have to do with it?"

"That is probably our conscious nagging us to return to her. So, it's a good thing we are heading back today."

"Do we have to wait until sunrise?" Hosperan asked.

"I don't think so. Let's get an early start if we're ready."

They both slung their sacks over their shoulders and grabbed their weapons off the wall. Hosperan attached a sword to his belt and his father put on his bow and quiver. Then they both grabbed a spear off the wall to use primarily as a walking stick. Hosperan's spear was straight and met his eye-line. His father's spear was waist high and thorny. Together, they extinguished the candles and headed outside. Hosperan's father held a torch in the air and led the way south toward Kilbo.

25

They were out of the village and under Jonnil Peak by the time the sun began to rise. Hosperan could not stop thinking about his confrontation with the fire beast in his dream.

"I don't think I am ready to fight the fire beast. I don't think I'm ready for 'When embers end,'" Hosperan said. "In my dream, I came face to face with the beast and I panicked."

"It was only a dream, Son. And you didn't have a plan."

"So, you have a plan?"

"Of course. As a village, we have multiple plans."

"Please share."

"Would that make you feel better?"

"Very much so," Hosperan replied.

"Well, I'll just tell you our primary plan. It is the best one, obviously. That's why it is the primary plan." Hosperan's father took a moment. They were walking on the southbound road through the hill country.

"I already told you the first part of the plan. Based on our studies and calculations it seems like the coastal villages are the last point of attack before the beast heads west over The Great Sea. We believe it lives somewhere due west of here."

"But you don't know for sure? How far do you think it is?"

"We don't know. A few years ago we sent a crew to the west to scout out the land of the fire beast. We wanted to know how long the trip was so we would know how many supplies to bring."

"Well?"

"They never returned."

"Oh."

"We like to believe they found the westward land and made a home there, and they will be waiting for us when we arrive. But it's likely they are now buried in the watery grave." Hosperan's father walked ahead and put his hands to his eyes. "Let's take a short break. I need to sit down for a second."

Hosperan found a small tree and decided to practice his spear throwing. His father had gone off over one of the small hills and was out of sight. Hosperan held the spear next to his ear and took a deep breath. He took aim and released.

Miss.

Just left of the tree.

He went and retrieved his spear and kept trying. He kept missing. On his last throw, he skimmed the side of the tree and the spearhead took some bark as it flew by.

"That's improvement," his father said, standing on the hill behind. "Ready to go?"

"Yeah," Hosperan said as he gathered his spear. "Are we making good time?"

"Pretty good, yeah. If we keep up this pace and get an early start tomorrow, we can be to Mount Kondor tomorrow night, and then get to Kilbo before sunset two days from now."

"That sounds good."

"Good. So, back to our plan."

"Oh, it's okay. We don't have to talk about it if you don't want to," Hosperan said.

"I appreciate that. But since you're fighting with us now, you need to be in the know about what's going on."

"Very well."

"So, the coastal attacks. The westward lands. The scout ships. The ships, yes. I bet you're wondering about the boats we're going to use to travel across The Great Sea."

"Oh yeah, you mentioned they're hidden somewhere?"

"Yes. In a cove up the coast. There's a cave only accessible by boat. There are three of them."

"In case the beast attacks Hofn."

"Exactly. Once we know the coast is clear, literally and figuratively, ha!"

"Oh my."

"That's great," his father was laughing at his own joke. "Once everything is clear, we'll sail the ships out of the cove and bring them down to the village to finish loading the supplies, and then we'll be off. The goal is to leave three days after the fire beast was last seen."

"Then what?"

"Sail until we reach land."

"What about the village? You're just going to leave it?" "We've made a deal with the Tillina tribe in the east. They built our ships, all four. And when we leave, we're giving them our village as payment."

"So, there's definitely no coming back then."

"There's no plan for that."

They walked in silence for the remaining part of the day. After walking in the dark for over an hour, Hosperan's father decided it was time to stop and camp for the night. They made a fire and ate some rabbit his father had caught with his bow.

"I hadn't thought about not coming back," Hosperan said.

"It's not out of the question, it just isn't an important part of our quest. There's no reason for us to plan a return. There's nothing else here for us."

"Except Mother."

His father didn't seem to acknowledge what Hosperan said.

"If we get to the land of the fire beast, and accomplish our task, no one will have any problem with you returning," his father said before standing to stomp the fire out. Once the embers turned cold, his father spoke again. "Let's get some sleep. We've got a long distance to cover tomorrow if we are going to make it to Mount Kondor by dusk. And I'll tell you the rest of the plan as we travel."

"The rest of the plan?"

"Well, yes. I've only told you up until sailing to the land of the fire beast. Tomorrow I will tell you how we kill the fire beast."

26

Again, Hosperan had the dreams.

And again, he could not fall back asleep.

His father was already awake when he woke this time. "The dreams again?" his father said.

"Yes," Hosperan replied. "You?"

"Yes, me too."

"I don't understand.'"

"I'm trying not to."

"What do you mean?"

"Son, it was not easy to leave you and your mother. There was no pleasure in it at all. It pained me on the first day and every day that followed. Until recently."

"What do you mean?"

"When we met in the cleft on Mount Kondor, the pain stopped. I had you. It was wonderful. It is wonderful." The first light began to rise over the eastern sky. "Shall we pack up and be on our way before I finish?"

"Okay."

They got up and dressed themselves and packed their beds. Then they stomped out the fire and put on their packs and continued their southbound journey.

"The pain, you said it stopped when we met again. Was there more?" Hosperan asked.

"Yes, I thought it was gone. Your presence was an overwhelming joy. I thought the pain to be gone for good."

"But then the dreams." Hosperan said.

"Yes," his father replied. "Your mother. That wound never healed. It was only overshadowed by your presence and then conversion to join us in our quest. Our reconciliation healed the wounds of abandonment one hundred times over. But it could never heal the wound of knowing I lied to your mother. I think that's why the dreams are back."

"And for me, too," Hosperan said. "Because of what I am about to do and the news I am about to share with her. I hope I can make peace with her."

"It's a heavy burden to bear, Son. To have someone you love hate you for choosing something else over them. Even though our quest is noble and true, not all will understand. And it's possible your mother will be one of those people."

Hosperan did not like the idea of hurting his mother. But he did not want to let her think he was dead either. He couldn't put her through that again. When she thought his father died she almost unraveled.

Not again.

"Let's walk in silence for a while, Son. We have important tasks ahead of us. It would be best to make sure we are focused." Hosperan looked up at his father and agreed. His father spoke for the last time while the sun was present.

"I will tell you the plan to defeat the beast when we make camp in the cleft at Mount Kondor tonight."

Hosperan spent the rest of that day thinking about what he would do if he actually met the beast face to face.

What would he do if he only had a sword?

How would he attack with a bow and some arrows? Was he a match for the beast with only a spear?

The seeds of doubt planted by the dreams were now close to bearing fruit. For the first time since he decided to join his father's cause, Hosperan was afraid. He knew the beast would make quick work of him. No shield could withstand the heat from that demonic fire. One exhale from the lungs of the beast and Hosperan would be reduced to ash.

And for what?

What if all the warriors in his father's village couldn't even make the beast bleed; not to mention take its life. They would all die there and no one would know. And he would never see his mother again.

Could he really leave her? Was he able to bear the weight of never seeing his own mother again? Especially knowing it was because of his choice. Would she be alright? Who would protect her in a time of trouble? She would have no one.

Hosperan figured he would be remembered as the chief who could have been, but he wasn't worried about chiefdom much. There was some comfort in knowing that his mother would be taken care of for being the widow of a former chief. But that was only a dwelling place and food rations. How would she get along mentally? She would not have anyone to talk to or be encouraged by.

Maybe he could convince her to come with them. They could fight the beast as a family. And they could be together. It would be perfect. It would be like a dream.

The good kind.

It was too good to be true.

Hosperan knew this was not a reality. His mother was a strong believer in the mission of the fire beast. She would not be easily swayed in the course of a day or two. She would need a sign. A sign like what Hosperan experienced. He began to pray that the gods would provide that for her.

They were making good time and arrived at the foot of Mount Kondor before the sun touched the horizon. His father took a moment to start a small fire and light two torches for them to use as they ascended the mountain pass in darkness.

As they arrived at the cleft, the memories of his friend began to arise inside Hosperan. They unpacked their things and made camp. As they were eating, Hosperan broke the silence.

"I must remember my friend. Can I do that now?"

"Of course, Son. What would you like to do?"

"Let me tell a story or two about him."

27

"When we were just boys, we used to play in the forest near Kilbo. We made a secret dwelling there. It was a castle and a ship and the back of the fire beast and other things from dreams. But Agur loved to come and try to steal our fun.

He always wanted what we had.

Gildor had run a small farm by himself since he was ten. He was teaching me about his crops, how to grow them, what the different types were, and everything like that. We were eating some of the different kinds when Agur and his friends showed up.

He said something like, 'Playtime is over. Give us whatever you're eating. Don't make us take it from you.' And Gildor was quick to reply, 'Fine, you can have it. Just don't take what's in that stone jar over there.'

This, of course, made Agur want it all the more. Which I later learned was the plan all along. So Agur and his friends took everything we were eating, including the stone jar, and left us alone. When they were gone, Gildor began to laugh uncontrollably. So, I asked him, 'What's the deal? We were just robbed.'

He said, 'Oh man, whew. That is going to be some funny stuff. I'm not worried about those crops. I've got plenty more. I had a good year. What I'm laughing about is that stone jar.'

'What's in it?' I asked.

'Poison plant. Ha! It won't do any permanent damage, but when they wake up in the morning, their tongues will be so swollen that they won't be able to keep them in their mouths.'"

"Well, was he right?" Hosperan's father said.

"He was spot on," Hosperan answered. "The next morning Agur and his friends looked like newborn calves searching for milk. It was great!"

Hosperan stuck his tongue out to imitate what Agur looked like after eating the poison plant. They both laughed as the fire burned in front of them. After the laughs died down, Hosperan spoke again.

"Just one more story."

"Tell as many as you'd like."

"I want to remember Gildor for his wit and cunning, but I also want to remember him for his compassion. There was a time, during this last harvest season, when I was helping him bring his crop into the village in order to sell and trade. He told me it had been a rough season.

'Not enough rain,' he said. 'Less than half the harvest I had last year.'

'What are you going to do?' I asked.

'Well, I've got enough stored from last year. It doesn't taste nearly as good. Nothing beats a fresh yield. Last year's stuff tastes like wet air and dirt.'

'Can you trade that instead of this fresh stuff?'

'I could, but they would only pay me half of what this is worth. And I don't blame them. It's terrible. But I should be able to get enough at the market to get thirty coins or so for this lot. That'll be enough to buy meat throughout the year when the hunters bring it in.'

When we arrived at the market to trade, there was an old woman with a cup begging for coins. She only had one leg and her hair was cut short. We traded the crop and Gildor made less than he expected. Only twenty-four coins. I started to head back to his house to return the barrows, but Gildor was kneeling, talking to the woman.

'What's your name?' he asked.

'Murida,' she replied.

'Nice to meet you, Murida. Are you waiting for someone?'

'No one left. Just me.'

'What do you mean?'

'Raiders take family. Take leg. No one left.'

'I'm sorry,' Gildor said.

And I was an idiot. I told Gildor that we should just leave and return his tools, then we could have dinner at my house. But Gildor wasn't concerned about that.

'Trade?' he asked the woman.

'With me?' she replied.

'Yes.'

'Necklace?' she said as she held up a leather necklace with a smooth stone tied to the end.

'Yes, twenty-four coins?'

The woman looked confused. She was slow in speech, but was well aware that this was not a fair trade. The necklace was old leather and a stone. Barely worth one coin if sold by a hard bargainer. But Gildor just wanted to help her.

'You sure? Too much,' she replied.

'Yes, I'm sure. Deal?'

'Okay,' she said. She lifted the necklace off her head and handed it to Gildor. And he handed her the coin bag.

'Thank you,' she said.

'Of course. Be well,' he replied."

Hosperan wiped the tears from his eye and turned from looking into the fire to looking over the surface of the fjord. He rubbed his thumb over the smooth stone hanging from his neck.

"Gildor taught me more about what it means to be chief than the elders or the record books ever did. When I asked him what he was going to eat this year, he told me he still had his dirt crop and that he guessed he would need to learn how to hunt for himself."

"Thank you for sharing, Son. You have honored your friend well. He sounds like a great man," his father said.

"He was a hero," Hosperan replied. "I'm going to go sit on the bank for a moment. I'll be back soon."

"Yes, of course. Take your time. I'll be here."

Hosperan left the warmth of the fire and walked to the edge of the fjord. There were many stories of his friend that surfaced in his mind. He recalled all of them that he could. He thanked the gods for his friend. He cried some more. And then he returned to his father.

"What we are about to do, to the fire beast, I'm doing it for all the people who will come after us," Hosperan said.

'Of course," his father replied.

"But I'm also doing it for those who have come before. I'm doing it for Gildor."

Hosperan sat down and wiped the tears from his eye. He focused on his father and continued to speak.

"So, how do we kill the beast?"

28

"Yes, the plan. Of course," his father replied. "The first part of the plan is to admit that you're scared. I'm scared. That thing is larger than any living thing I've ever seen and it breathes death hotter than any fire we could ever make. So, yeah. I'm afraid. Are you afraid, Son?"

"Very much so. I'm doubting if I made the right decision."

"Well, good. Then you aren't a crazy, thrill-seeking radical. You're normal."

"What do you mean?"

"Normal people don't delight in taking part in a battle where they are incredibly outmatched. Your reaction, and mine, of being afraid, is normal."

"We can't fight if we're afraid."

"Sure we can, we just do it afraid."

"Okay, well, that helps I think. I'm glad it's not just me," Hosperan said.

"Me too," his father replied. "So, step one complete. The rest of the plan is not exactly linear. There are just a few things that need to happen, but they can happen in any order."

"What do you mean?"

"Hmm, where to start. Well, I already told you how we're going to get to the beast's homeland."

"The ships. In the cove."

"Yes, exactly. Those ships play a major role in our plan to defeat the beast. We need to get the beast to attack our ships, because that will mean it is fighting over water. That will be important later."

"Okay, what else?"

"We're at an incredible disadvantage since we can't fly."

"So, we need to take out its wings."

"Exactly. We've developed a new type of arrow and spear. It's the walking stick I've been using."

His father stood and walked over to where their packs were sitting and grabbed the spear. He brought it back over to the fire and handed it to Hosperan.

"See how the staff has jagged points sticking out?"

"Like thorns."

"Yes, like thorns. We call it the rose weapon," his father said. "The goal is to not only pierce the beast's wing, but to actually get the spear and arrows stuck in the wings. And then, hopefully, the force of the up and down motion on the wings will cause it to move and tear more of the wing. The ultimate goal is to render the wings useless. We're pretty sure we just need to make one wing unusable and that'll be enough to keep the beast from flying. Still, we'll try to fill both wings with roses."

"So that's how the sea comes into play. You're going to try and drown the beast."

"Exactly. We tried to think through every scenario and tactic, but this seemed best. And once the beast is in the water, we'll ram the bow of our ships through its body."

"And that'll destroy your ships," Hosperan said.

"No return plan, remember?" his father replied.

"I understand. There is only one plan. Kill the fire beast."

"Exactly."

"So, it seems like the only part of the plan that is missing is getting the beast to the water. What if it lives far inland?"

"We've considered this and have not come to a great solution. Right now, there's a select group of our bravest warriors, The Vaskr Five, and they are going to find the beast and lead it back to the coast. They'll aggravate the beast and use themselves as bait to lure it to our ambush. They'll not likely survive this kind of frontline warfare."

"I see," Hosperan said. He was still holding the rose weapon in his hands. "Do the rose weapons fly true? Since they have the extra weight."

"Unfortunately, no. That was one of the sacrifices required. It's still accurate though. Let me put it this way, you probably couldn't hit a specific spot on a cow from three hundred paces, but you could hit the cow."

"That's not too bad then," Hosperan replied. "Good enough to pierce a wing."

"That's exactly right. Our weapon smiths worked tirelessly to try and arrange the thorns in a way that did not hinder the flight pattern. They did an incredible job."

"I'd like to test it out some when we get back to the village. See how it flies."

"Of course," his father said.

"I'd also like to hear some stories from the different Nights of Fire you lived through."

THE ROSE WEAPON

"Are you more interested in learning about me or the fire beast?" his father joked.

"Yes," Hosperan replied with a smile.

"Good answer, ha!" His father relaxed himself and, by the look on his face, began to recall some of his favorite memories. "Okay, well, I'll start by saying the beast is unpredictable. During my second Night of Fire, my first as chief, I was only a little older than you are now. We had the usual festival and everyone was preparing for the arrival of the beast. And it came later than ever before. We waited and waited. We said the daily prayers and gave the offerings, but nothing happened for the longest time."

"What was everyone in the village thinking?" Hosperan asked.

"They were split. The older folks thought this to be a sign the gods had disowned us. And the younger were secretly relieved."

"Which side were you on?"

"The relieved side," his father answered. "Have you heard the story about how my arm got this way?"

"Yes, the storyteller told it at the last festival."

"Well, ever since that first Night of Fire, when I saw that toddler trapped under flame, I knew this could not be ordained by the gods. Babies and children being sacrificed? It was too evil. I was glad to become chief so I could protect our people from the beast without them even knowing it. But it took me until my second Night of Fire, the one I was just talking about, to get the idea of building the strongholds in the middle of every house."

"And you called them prayer rooms."

"It was an easy sell, because when the beast finally did come, it flew over briefly and then moved on. I

113

convinced the elders that it was because we had not prayed enough. They agreed and the prayer rooms were built. It was great."

"That's brilliant."

"Thank you, Son. It wasn't enough though."

"Why not?"

"I was never at peace knowing that the beast was killing other innocent people around the world. After the prayer rooms were completed, I started developing the plan to destroy the fire beast. I was going to fake my own death the next Night of Fire. I knew that if I told everyone what I was doing, it would make my decisions invalid. The prayer strongholds might be abandoned. And I knew your mother would be taken care of if I became a sacrifice."

"So, what happened? You didn't follow through because I wasn't born yet."

"I was too scared. The fire beast came early, and with twice the heat and destruction. We weren't ready. I ran to our prayer room with your mother and hid until it was all over. We lost a lot of good people that night. The elders viewed the mass casualties as a direct success of the prayer rooms."

"That's terrible," Hosperan whispered.

"It was. And it was the thing that actually put me over the edge. I knew this was bigger than me and my fears. I had to kill the beast. But now I didn't have a way to die with honor. I was trying to come up with a new plan, and then you were born."

"Sorry about that," Hosperan laughed.

"Yeah, way to go. Delaying the destruction of the greatest evil in this world."

"I guess I've got that kind of charm."

"You definitely do. You were incredible. It made my decision to leave so much more difficult. It's not that I didn't love your mother, I do, but knowing how difficult and painful your life would be growing up in the shadow of a sacrificed chief...it almost made me stay."

Hosperan got up from his log and went over and sat down next to his father. He put his arm around his father and held him close.

"You did the right thing, Father," Hosperan said. Tears began to roll down his father's face. This caused Hosperan to cry as well.

"You have no idea how much it means to hear you say that. I love you, Son."

"I love you too."

They sat and hugged for a few more moments. The fire continued to flicker and the haze continued to hover over the hot spring. Hosperan was still without one eye. His friend had still been killed by a pack of lynx. He was still set to become the chief of Kilbo. And the fire beast was still coming.

Even still, Hosperan couldn't remember a better night in his life.

They stayed up late telling stories about their past that neither of them were present for. The next morning, because of the lack of sleep, the sun rose long before they did. Once they finally woke, it did not take long to get breakfast and get moving. They continued southward on the mountain pass toward Kilbo. They were to the point on the pass where the snow melted and the dirt path appeared.

"You know, I haven't asked you what you want for your birthday tomorrow."

"I don't need anything," Hosperan replied.

"Oh, come on. Everyone loves presents."

"I can't focus on that right now, Father."

"Very well."

"Are you just going to wait in the forest then?" Hosperan asked.

"I think so, if that's alright with you," his father replied.

"Of course. I'll try not to keep you waiting long."

"Don't rush it, Son. I can wait as long as you need me to. You only get to say your last goodbye once."

"I don't want to be seen by anyone else, though."

"That's a good plan."

It did not take long for them to descend to the bottom of the mountain, and reach the final stretch of road that led through the forest, and to the northern edge of Kilbo. They stopped and had a late lunch before making the rest of their journey.

"I forgot to ask you how you and Svana are doing?" his father asked as he cut a piece of loaf for his son.

"Me and Svana? How did you… "

"Oh, come on, Son. Everyone in the village has known how much you care about each other since you were infants," his father replied. "Did something happen?"

"I didn't know it was that obvious. Nothing happened. We're…still together."

"You better make sure to pay her a visit, too, while you're saying your goodbyes."

Hosperan didn't reply. He didn't finish his lunch either. How could he have forgotten about Svana? He felt sick to his stomach with shame.

They packed up their meal and made their way into the forest. The sun was beginning to set in front of them as they entered the thick of the trees.

"Do you smell that?" Hosperan's father said.

"What?" Hosperan said. His father's question shocked him from his regretful thoughts. "Smoke and cinders? Is it from our clothes?" Hosperan replied.

"No, I don't think so. It's too strong," his father said as he surveyed the area. "I think it's getting stronger too."

They came to a clearing in the forest that silenced both of them. Hosperan knew his home was just on the other side of the clearing. That knowledge frightened him the most.

A cloud of smoke the size of his village was ascending into the heavens.

29

Hosperan and his father took off in a sprint toward the village. Hosperan's mind was racing faster than his feet. He could not face the beast now. He wasn't ready. He did not have the villagers from Hofn with him. They did not have the boats. He only had one rose weapon. It was too soon.

His mother.

He had to find her first. He needed to tell her the truth. He needed her to know that he was still alive and that he had found purpose and meaning in life. He needed to apologize that his new life might make her sad. He didn't want her to be sad.

And Svana.

When they arrived at the edge of the village, people were running around screaming. Hosperan saw his cousin, Agur and ran after him and grabbed him by the arm.

"Hosperan, you're..." Agur said.

"Yes, I'm alive. I'm here."

"Your eye."

"Never mind that. What's going on? Where is the beast?"

"The beast? The beast isn't here."

"What?" Hosperan asked. "The fire? The smoke?"

"Raiders from Sokn-Akr. They heard our chief was away." With this, Agur loosed himself from Hosperan's grip and ran off into the woods. Hosperan took a moment to orient himself.

Raiders.

Not the fire beast.

He wasn't sure if this was good news. Before he could decide, a stranger ran toward him with an axe drawn. Hosperan fumbled to get his rose spear loose from his pack. An arrow flew through the neck of the axe man. He fell to the ground. Hosperan's father came running up to his son with his bow drawn.

"You're going to have to be a bit quicker than that, Son. Are you ready?"

"Yes, yes. Sorry. It's just…raiders. No fire beast."

"And there won't be a fire beast if we don't make it out of this. Come on, let's find your mother."

"Yes, of course. Okay," Hosperan said as he gathered himself. "To the house then."

"It is the same house, I assume," his father replied.

"Yes, this way."

They both ran toward the biggest house in the village. It was in view, but nearly two hundred paces away. This is where Hosperan lived his entire life. He never thought he would be in the house with his father again. But his dream was stunted when a group of raiders burst out of the front door of the house carrying a woman toward The Great Hall.

His mother.

"Stop!" Hosperan yelled. His father drew his bow and began taking down the savages. Their archer retaliated and Hosperan and his father were forced into shelter.

Hosperan heard a scream coming from the woods. He looked around the side of the house where they were hiding and saw Svana being carried toward the forest.

"Svana," Hosperan yelled. The raiders turned and aimed their bows in the direction of the voice. His father pulled him back.

"You're not very good at this fighting thing," his father said.

"It's Svana. They've taken her into the forest," Hosperan replied.

"What do you want to do?"

"We can't just hide."

"We're no good to them if we're dead. We need to work together and take out their archer first. How fast are you?"

"I don't know."

"Well, if you run across the road and get the archer's attention, I'll be able to take him out. I only need a few seconds. Can you do that?"

"Yes. Yes. Okay, yes."

"And then we go for your mother or Svana?" his father asked. Hosperan hesitated. He closed his eye and covered his face with his hands. After a moment, he replied.

"Mother."

"Okay, on my count. Don't get shot," his father said. "Three, two, one, go!" Hosperan took off across the open road. He waited for an enemy arrow to strike him.

But it didn't happen.

He made it across the road and behind the edge of a house. By the time he looked back, his father was already standing up and running toward the mob that had kidnapped their loved one. Hosperan joined him.

"What happened?" Hosperan asked.

"I told you I only needed a second. But now we're going to have to see some of those hand-to-hand combat skills at work. Let's go save your mother."

Hosperan placed the rose spear in the sling on his back and unsheathed his sword. There were people battling all around them. A house across the street had just collapsed, followed by the sound of screams.

The enemy raiders ran toward the two of them. Hosperan counted five or six. They were outnumbered, but he never felt they were going to die there. The fighting style of the enemy was sloppy and undisciplined. The opponent went for a killing blow early, and Hosperan capitalized on the mistake and wedged his sword into the exposed areas. He and his father made quick work of the ragtag group, but when they had slain the last, Hosperan's mother was nowhere to be found.

"We need to let your soldiers do the fighting here. This isn't our battle. We need to find your mother."

"Yes, yes. You're right." Hosperan found himself agreeing with his mouth, but feeling unsure in his mind. He did need to find his mother; that was the first priority. "Let's go check their ships in the bay."

They both ran behind the houses in order to try and avoid any unnecessary detection. They moved slower, but they did not have to engage in battle. They came to the last house before the coast and peered around it. The sun was setting into the ocean. The burning homes took over as the primary light source.

"Do you see your mother?"

"It's hard to tell. I don't think so," Hosperan replied. "I don't see anyone on board."

"Why do you think they're here?" his father asked.

"I ran into Agur when we first entered the village and he said the raiders heard the village was without a chief. I don't know how the word got out," Hosperan replied.

"It's not your fault, Son. It's the elders' fault. You're not even chief yet. They should have plans for this. They should be able to defend the village."

Hosperan could see his father was getting angry, so he decided to change the subject. He didn't feel like the attack was his fault. The elders had never taught him how to make decisions. They always said he could be heard when he was officially chief. This was his village, but only by birth.

"Let's split up to cover more ground," Hosperan said.

"Are you sure, son?"

"Yes, I'm ready to fight now. It just took me a second to get my mind ready. The village has changed some since you were last here, so I'll search the village if you want to check the forest."

"What about the raider ship?" his father asked.

"It doesn't look like anyone is on it, see?" Hosperan said as he pointed toward the bay.

"Strange," his father replied. "Well, let's meet at the house when we're done."

"Good idea."

"Be safe," his father said as he raised his arm in the air and curved his fingers in the shape of a C.

"You too." Hosperan returned the gesture and they knelt with their hands interlocked for a few seconds before his father ran off toward the trees.

Hosperan took a moment to try and decide where to check first.

The Great Hall.

He knew this is where the elders kept the gold and the other valuable items. Hosperan snuck back behind the houses where they had just come. He stopped as he reached the town square and checked the crossroads to see if there was anyone present. There was one person.

But he was no longer alive.

One of his fellow villagers had been killed by the raiders and left to die in the street. Hosperan wanted to give this stranger a proper burial, but he knew there was no time. He needed to find his mother. She was in danger. He made a vow to himself that he would come back and honor this man. But for now, he made his way around houses and into the courtyard of The Great Hall.

As Hosperan hopped the fence and planted his foot in the yard, he felt the ground tremble beneath him. His ears throbbed from a devilish cry he hadn't heard in ten years.

The fire beast.

30

The cry echoed off the mountains to the north and invaded every corner of Kilbo.

"No. Not yet," Hosperan said to himself. But it was.

The beast followed its cry and passed over the village just above the treetops. It spread its wings and covered the length of four houses. Its skin was blacker than the night sky above it. The sun was gone, but there were two light sources. The fire from the burning houses. And the fire rushing from the mouth of the beast.

Raiders burst through the doors of The Great Hall. They were carrying gold and precious stones. They were not celebrating. Half of them took off in the direction of the ship and the other half took off toward the forest. Hosperan took this opportunity to search for his mother inside.

The Great Hall was burning on the outside, but the inside was without flame. This building had been constructed with double stone to protect it from any threats; including the fire from the beast.

"Mother!" Hosperan shouted. "Mother, it's Hosperan." No reply.

He checked the meeting room. No one there.

He checked the offices. No one there.

He checked the treasury. No one there.

The raiders left a few things behind. On the wall of the treasury hung his father's shield that had been recovered after his apparent death. Hosperan did not think twice before grabbing his father's item. He fastened the shield to his forearm and left the building.

He headed toward town square in order to check the markets and neighboring houses. As he headed toward the square, he could see the beast circling the northern edge of the village to adjust its route. Then the beast flew low and released fire, followed by the cries of men.

A distraction.

Hosperan hoped the men acting as bait were the raiders and not his fellow villagers. He tried not to think about it. He had a small window with the beast distracted and he still needed to find his mother. Once he arrived at the square, he saw his father running back from the direction of the forest.

"Father," Hosperan shouted. His father changed course and headed for Hosperan. His father's hands were pink with dried blood. They hid under the wings of the bronze fire beast in the middle of the square. "Any luck?" Hosperan asked.

"Just raiders in the forest."

"Fifl," Hosperan cursed.

"I'm sure you've seen that the situation has changed a bit. We have to hurry and find your mother, and then get back to Hofn so we can follow close behind the beast."

"I know, I know. I couldn't find her in The Great Hall," Hosperan said.

"I see you found my shield, though."

"Yes, I thought you might want it back," Hosperan said as he began to hand the shield to his father.

"You keep it," his father insisted. "Birthday present."

Hosperan held the shield in his hand and didn't say anything. He was glad to have it. He had dreamt about wielding it for as long as he could remember.

"It looks like the beast is distracted with those raiders," his father said. "Let's use that to our advantage. Back to the house? We've checked everywhere else."

"Yes, let's go. She has to be there. When the fire beast comes, everyone runs to their homes religiously. I bet that's where she went, if she got free."

They both took off running up the main street and then turned south. The chief's house was at the end of the street. They were nearly there when a rushing wind knocked them off their feet. The dirt kicked up and mixed with smoke. Hosperan looked up from the ground, but could no longer see his house. The ground shook violently for a moment.

The dust cleared.

The fire beast had landed on Hosperan's house.

31

"No!" Hosperan cried.

The beast bent its head down low and released a torrent of flames directly at them. Hosperan's father grabbed his son's arm and pulled them both to safety on the side of a house. The fire rushed by and consumed the front of the house where they were hiding.

"Listen, Son. It's just the two of us. The raiders are gone and the villagers are all in their homes."

"We need to check the house for Mother," Hosperan cried.

"We will," his father said. "But we'll never get there with the beast guarding it." His father leaned Hosperan forward and grabbed the rose spear from his son's back. "Time to test your skills."

"What? I can't? What is one spear going to do? This isn't the plan."

"The plan changes. This is all we've got. Here's what we're going to do. I'm going to use my bow to get the beast's attention and make it chase me. I'm going to run back toward the village square. Once the coast is clear, check the rubble for your mother. And if you see an opportunity to use the rose weapon, take it."

"But..." Hosperan began to argue.

"There's no time, Son. Stay alive. Go back to Hofn and tell them what happened. Lead them to the beast's homeland. Make the beast pay. You can do it." After his father said this, he kissed Hosperan on the forehead and pulled an arrow from his quiver and ran into the street.

His father released one arrow toward the beast and took off toward the square.

Hosperan couldn't see where the arrow had hit, but he knew it made contact because the beast recoiled for a moment. The beast extended its wings and leaned forward toward Hosperan's father. Its wings began to move up and down. The rose weapon was still in Hosperan's hands. He took a deep breath, gripped the spear, and raised it to the side of his head. The dust and smoke began to swirl as the beast started to take flight. Seconds later, the massive creature was heading in his direction. Hosperan would only have a few seconds to release the rose weapon.

He ran into the street and launched the weapon straight into the air.

The fire beast flew overhead and caught the rose weapon with its wing. The spear pierced a hole in the beast's left wing and remained lodged.

Red rain fell from the sky moments before the beast itself. The piercing of the beast's wing caused it to lose its balance, and do a corkscrew crash landing on top of multiple houses. The beast's head rested on the ground to Hosperan's left. The tip of the rose weapon was colored a shimmering blood-red.

By this time, his father was running toward the beast with bow and arrow in hand. Hosperan saw his father release an arrow and wedge it directly into the beast's right eye.

The head of the beast raised into the air immediately, accompanied by a painful cry that Hosperan had never heard before. The fire beast let out a stream of fire into the air and then began to move its wings up and down. It was clearly favoring the wounded wing. The beast struggled to get airborne. This gave Hosperan and his father time to hide behind one of the few standing houses across the street.

"I think we…" Hosperan began to say.

"No, son. The arrow can barely pierce the beast's eye. It could not reach the brain from that distance."

"But, it's leaving."

Hosperan pointed at the beast as it began to fly higher into the air. It was struggling to fly with the wounded wing, but it was still able to carry itself through the air. It retreated west over the ocean. Hosperan and his father waited to let their guard down until they could no longer see the beast. Then Hosperan spoke.

"Mother…"

32

Hosperan ran toward the half-collapsed house. He could see people coming out of the few houses that were still standing. He did not care if they saw him. He only cared about one thing.

"Mother!" he cried again, as he came to the burning house. "I have to go in," Hosperan said.

"Let's go, quickly. I don't know how long it will remain standing."

The door, along with the front of the house, had been crushed when the beast landed. They walked into the front opening and began searching for any signs of life.

"Mother! Mother! It's Hosperan!"

They both began lifting fallen roof beams. They made their way to the prayer room in the middle of the house. The stone room had been reduced to rubble. The rubble was resting on his mother.

"Mother, no. No! Are you okay? Mother," Hosperan knelt beside his mother. Her legs were pinned under stone. Blood was coming out of a deep head wound. His father put two fingers on her neck.

"Her heart is beating. Barely." As he was saying this, her eyelids retracted. She was awake for a moment before closing her eyes again.

"Mother," Hosperan said through tears. "We need to get you out of here."

"Let's lift these stones."

They got to their feet and began moving the stones off their loved one. After a few moments, she was free. Her legs were bloodied and bruised.

"We need to get out of here before the whole place comes down," Hosperan's father said.

"I'll grab Mother," Hosperan said.

"Son, let me carry her out of here. You go find a medicine man."

"Okay. Okay," Hosperan replied, before comprehending what his father had just said.

He ran out of the house. Raknar looked down at his wife. Tears fell from his eyes as he bent down and wrapped his arms around her. He carried her out of the house for the last time. He tried to be gentle to reduce the pain. When they made it out of the house, a large crowd had gathered. Hosperan came running onto the scene with the village medicine man. Raknar laid his wife on the ground.

"She's still breathing," the medicine man said, as he attended to Hosperan's mother. "But she's lost a lot of blood."

"Is she going to make it?" Hosperan asked.

33

Before he got a reply, a man stepped forward in front of the crowd. He was dressed in the elder attire.

"Hosperan. Raknar. This is quite a surprise," Ragnhild said loud enough so everyone could hear. "What are you…"

"No. I'll do the talking," Hosperan said. He dried his tears. "Look at this destruction. Where are the rest of the people in the village? Why are they not here? You would think they wouldn't miss seeing a man come back from the dead. I'll tell you why they aren't here," Hosperan had walked up to Ragnhild and was standing face-to-face with him at this point. "Because they're dead."

"Honorable sacrifices," Ragnhild interjected.

"No, no! A sacrifice has to cost something. The death of these people cost you nothing. You could care less. You didn't have to give up anything. The gods don't want our lives. They want our honor and respect. They want our praise. They don't want us to die, they created us! They want us to live in a way that gives them glory."

"What is this nonsense? The gods don't care about what we do," the elder replied.

"How could they not care? When have you ever created something and not cared about it? It can't be," Hosperan gathered himself and spoke loud enough for everyone to hear. "My father has helped my understanding. He has given me knowledge about the gods. The gods care about us. They don't want us to die by the breath of the beast. That's why we are going to kill the beast."

The crowd gasped together.

"Ha, you're out of your mind," Ragnhild said.

"Join us. Come with us to do something that actually matters. Come help us kill the beast and therefore save the lives of the thousands who will come after we are gone. Who's with us?"

No one in the crowd moved. The villagers looked at each other and whispered, but no one joined Hosperan and his father.

"You see? If you were speaking truth, these people would follow you. But no one wants to chase after this illusion."

"They would rather live peacefully in a lie," Hosperan replied. "Fine, you've made your decision. I can't blame you. I didn't believe at first either. But when we return with the head of the beast on a pole, then you'll know what I have spoken today is the truth. You'll know the gods have ordained our victory over the beast."

The medicine man spoke as Hosperan finished. "She's waking up."

34

"Mother," Hosperan cried as he fell to his knees. "I'm sorry. I'm sorry." But his mother's focus was on the other man standing over her. The look in her eyes went from anger to confusion to sadness to surprise to gladness in just a few seconds.

"I'm sorry too," his father said as he knelt beside her. "I should have told you. I wasn't honest with you. I didn't trust you. I should have just told you the truth. Please forgive me."

Hosperan's mother tried to speak, but no words came out. She closed her eyes.

"Mother," Hosperan said as he put his hand under her head. Her eyes opened again and she looked at her son. The disappointment Hosperan felt flowing from her eyes pierced his soul.

He wept.

"I'm sorry, Mother. I should've been here. To protect you. To keep you safe. I should've asked you to come with me. I want you to find what I have found. Mother, I've found great meaning for my life. I finally feel like I'm doing something that matters." Hosperan paused. "But at what cost? This is too much. Please forgive me."

More villagers had gathered around them at this point. Hosperan continued to weep beside his mother. He wasn't sure how much time had passed, but he knew it was too fast. The most important moments in life never seem to last long enough. As he was kneeling there holding his mother, he felt her reach up and put her hands over his wounded eye and then down to his cheeks. She closed her eyes, but her breathing remained steady.

"I'm sorry, Son. But we need to go," his father said, breaking the silence.

"Is she going to be okay?" Hosperan asked the man bandaging his mother's wounds.

"I don't think she'll be able to walk again, but I've managed to stop the bleeding," he replied. "She has passed out again, but I think she'll make it."

Hosperan was comforted in the prognosis. But, it didn't make his next decision any easier. He knelt down once more and kissed his mother's forehead. "I love you, Mother." He lifted the old leather necklace off his shoulders and placed it around her neck. Tears fell from his face to hers. He stood up and faced a crowd twice the size of the one he had spoken to just moments before. He hugged his father.

After the short embrace, they walked past Ragnhild and through the crowd of people. Once they were out of earshot from the crowd, his father spoke.

"We need to head back to Hofn."

"We are," Hosperan said.

"We're going the wrong way," his father replied.

"No, we're not," Hosperan said as they walked west toward the shore. He pointed toward the raider ship that was abandoned in the bay. "We'll take the ship up the coast and make it to Hofn in a quarter of the time. And then we'll have an extra ship for the journey."

"Good thinking," his father said. "We're actually doing it."

His father wiped his face, grabbed his son's hand and lifted it into the air and cried out, "When embers end."

Hosperan replied, "When embers end."

THE ROSE WEAPON

HOSPERAN WILL RETURN.

ABOUT THE AUTHOR

F.C. Shultz is an author from the American Midwest who did not begin writing fiction until his early twenties when the stories of Ray Bradbury grabbed hold of him and never let go. He likes to introduce one fantasy element into an otherwise realistic world and see what happens. It has been great fun so far.

He lives with his wife, Sammi, and his cat, Batman in Joplin, Missouri.

Made in the USA
Columbia, SC
26 September 2022